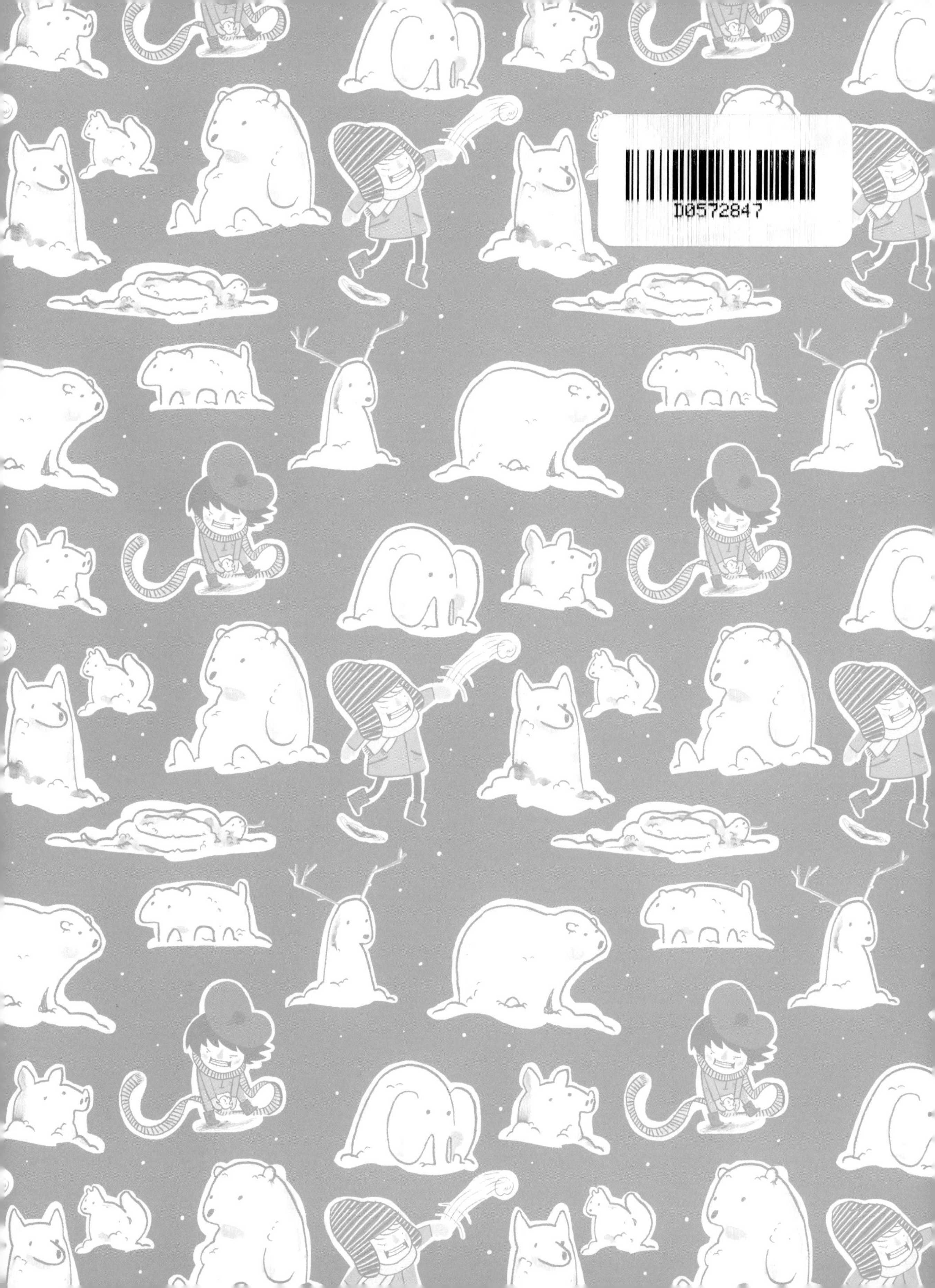

LIVI & NATE

Kalle Hakkola · Mari Ahokoivu

LIVI & NATE

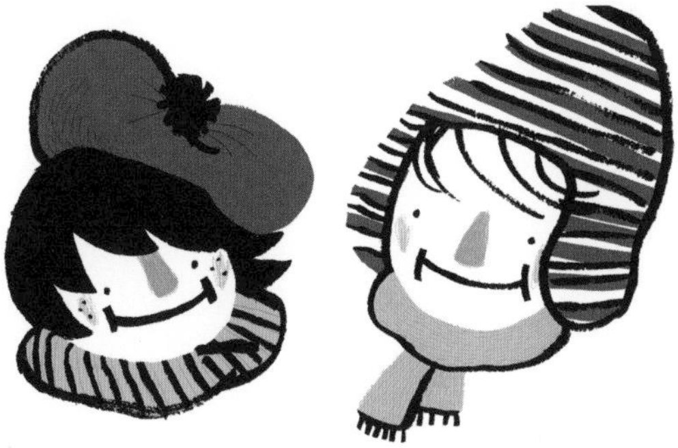

Translated by Owen F. Witesman

Owlkids Books

MEET THE FAMILY

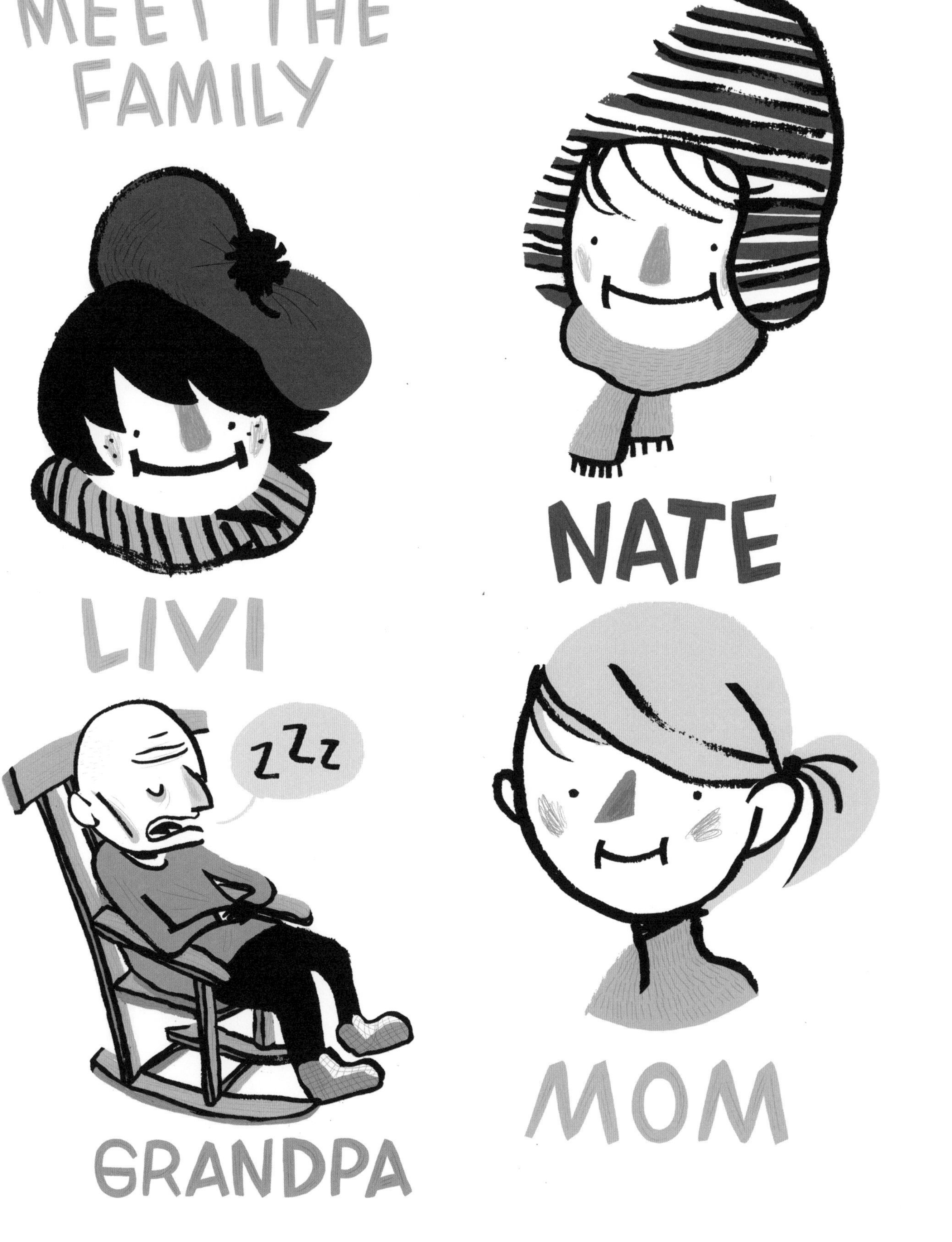
NATE
LIVI
ZZZ
MOM
GRANDPA

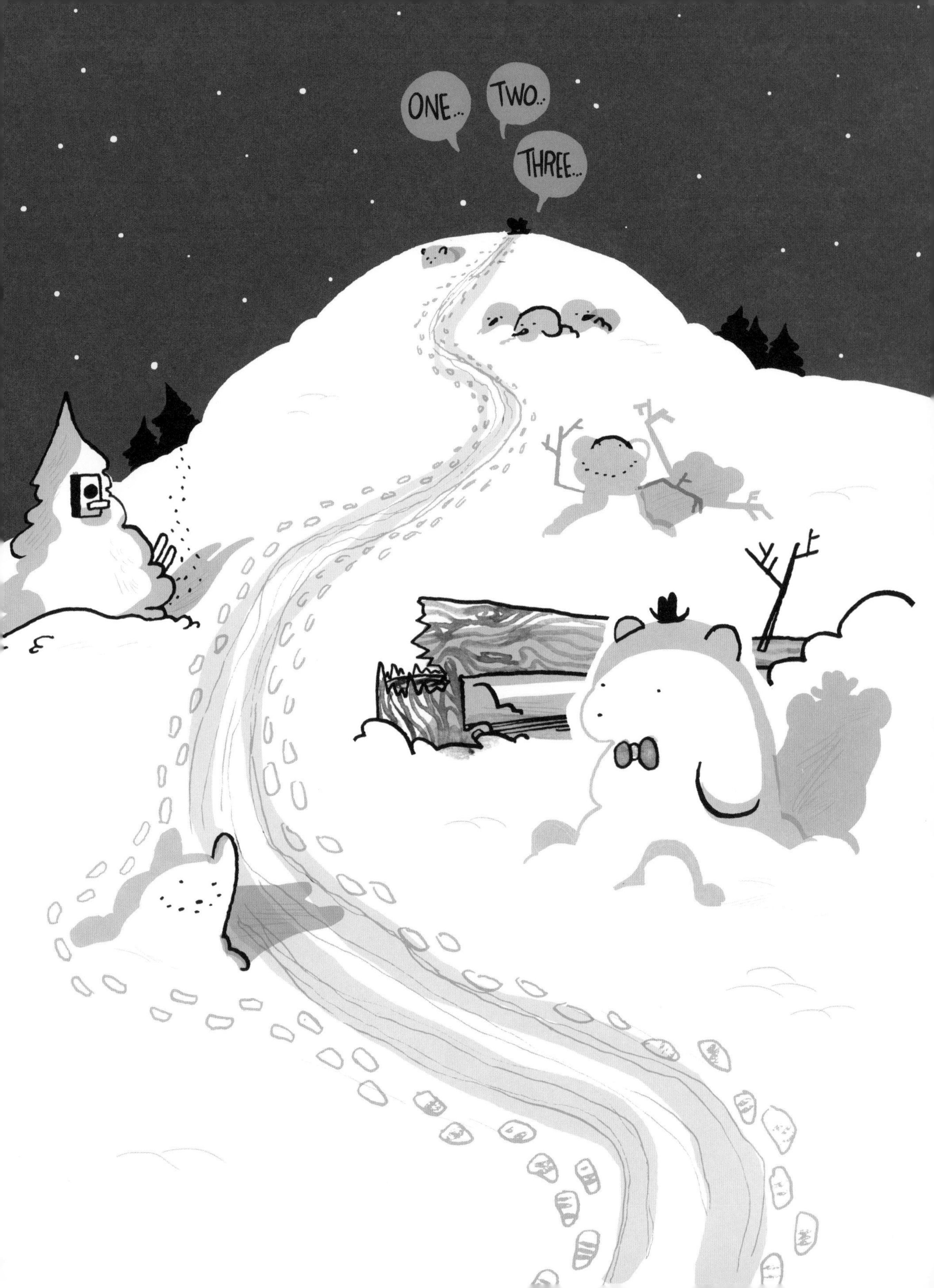
ONE...
TWO..
THREE...

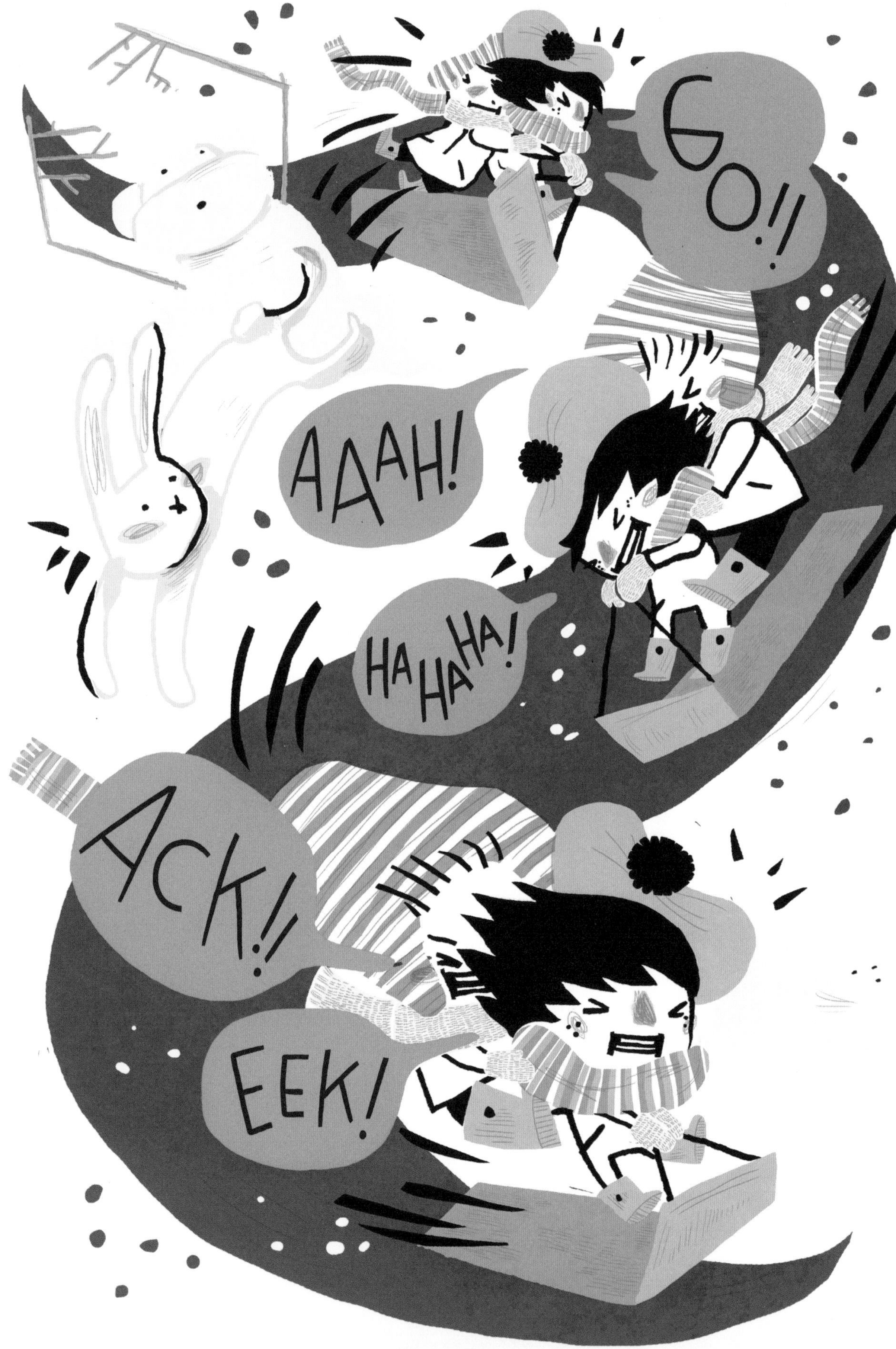
GO!!
AAAH!
HA HA HA!
ACK!!
EEK!

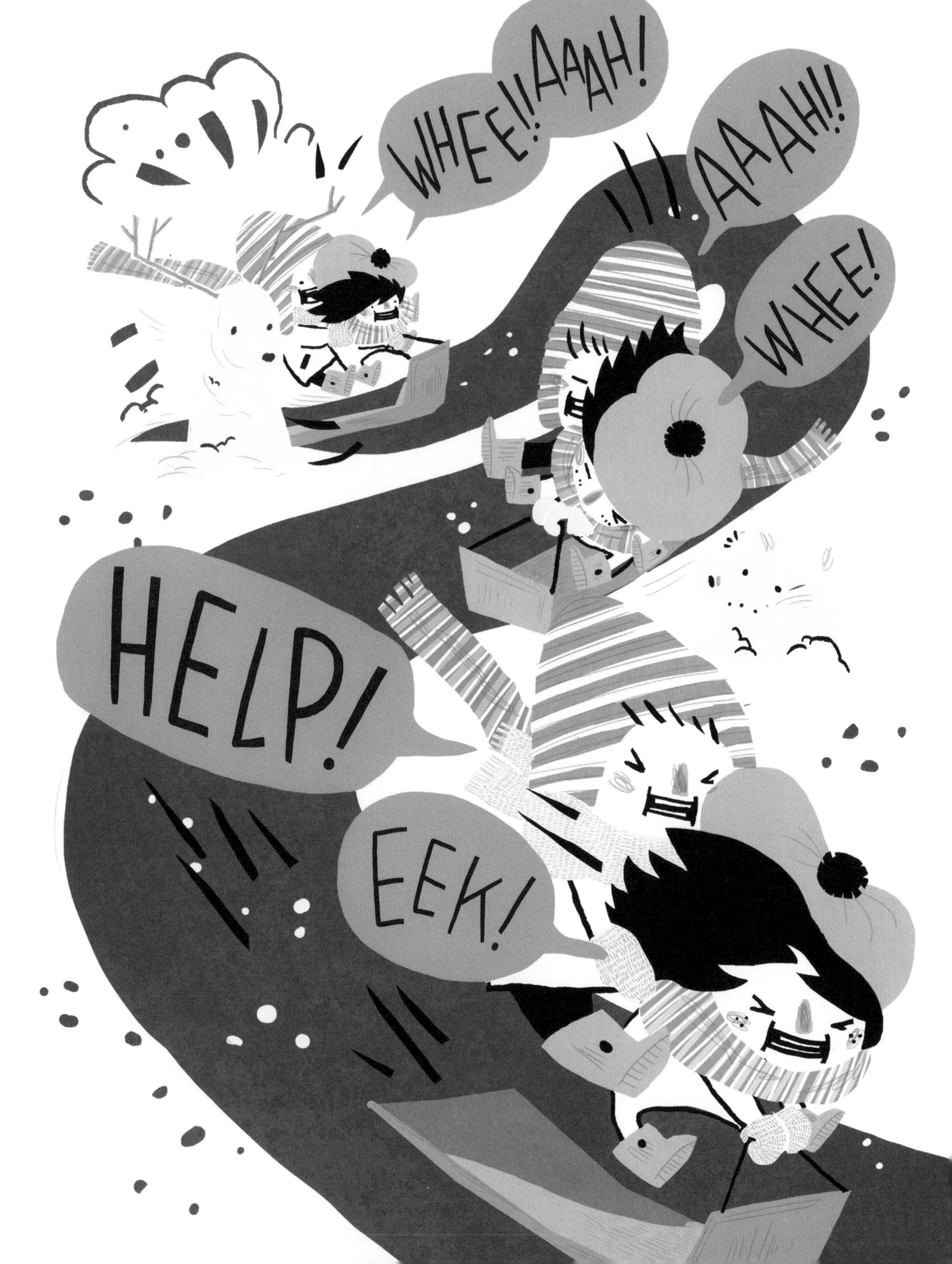
WHEE!
AAAH!
AAAH!!
WHEE!
HELP!
EEK!

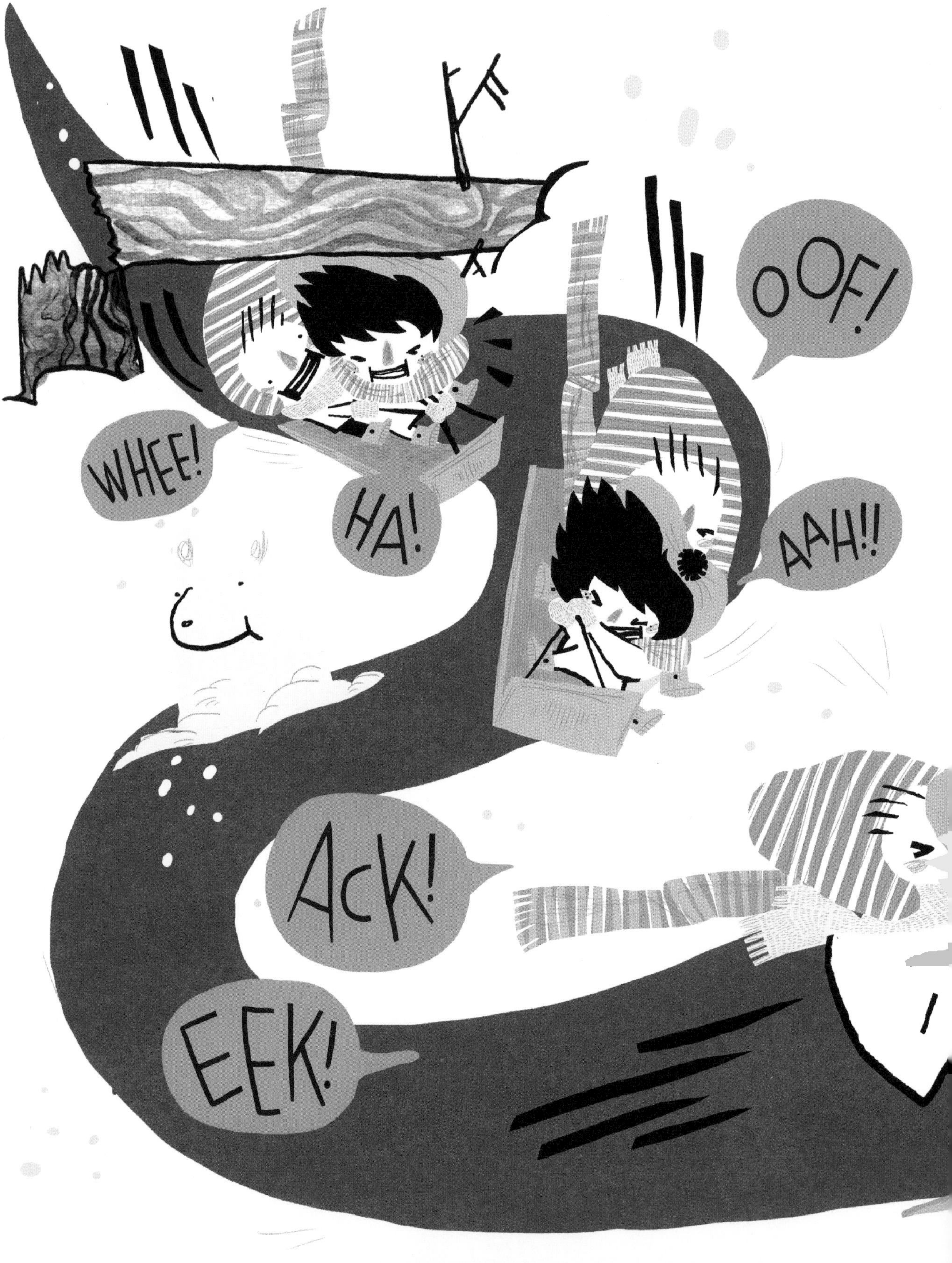
WHEE!
HA!
OOF!
AAH!!
ACK!
EEK!

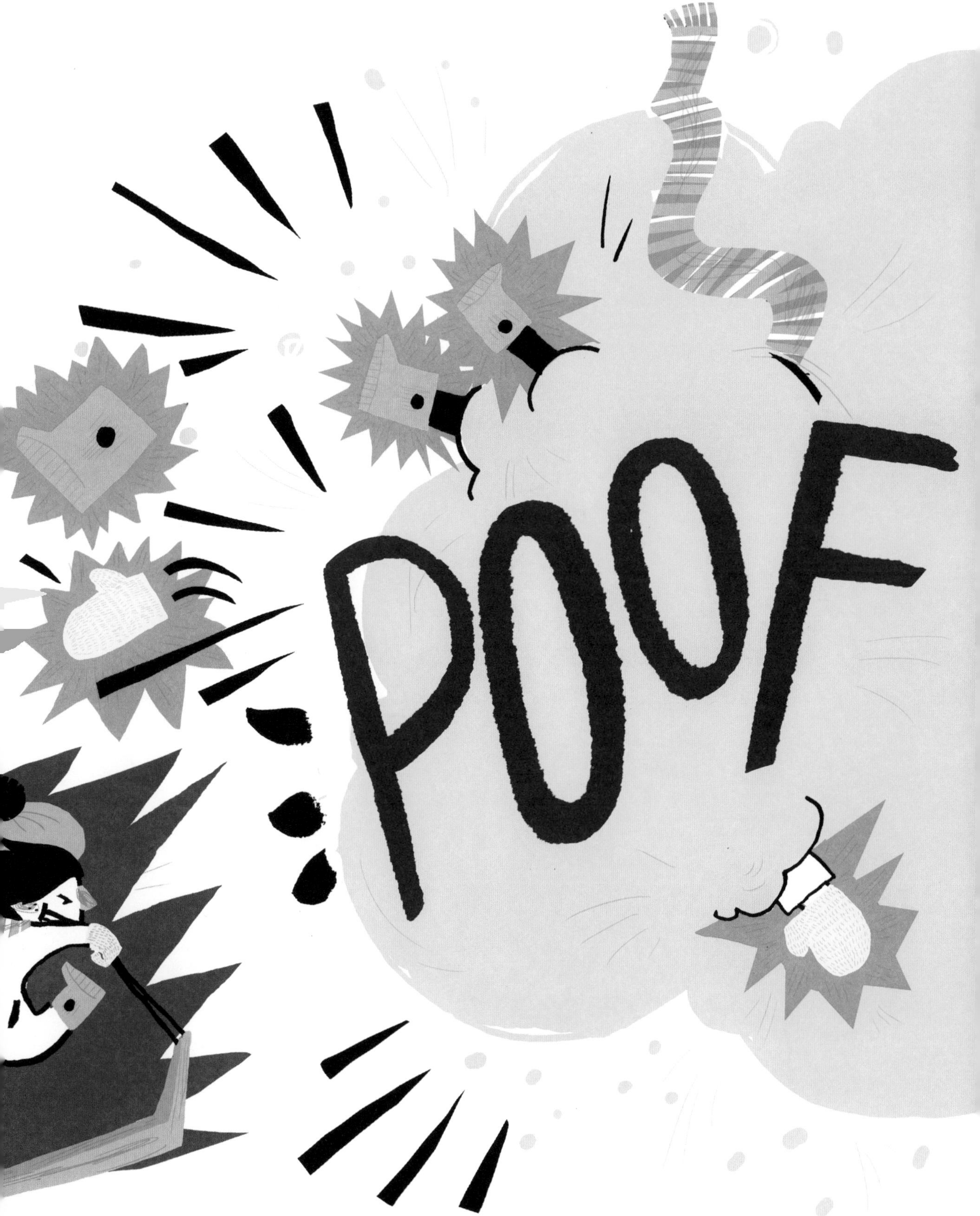
POOF

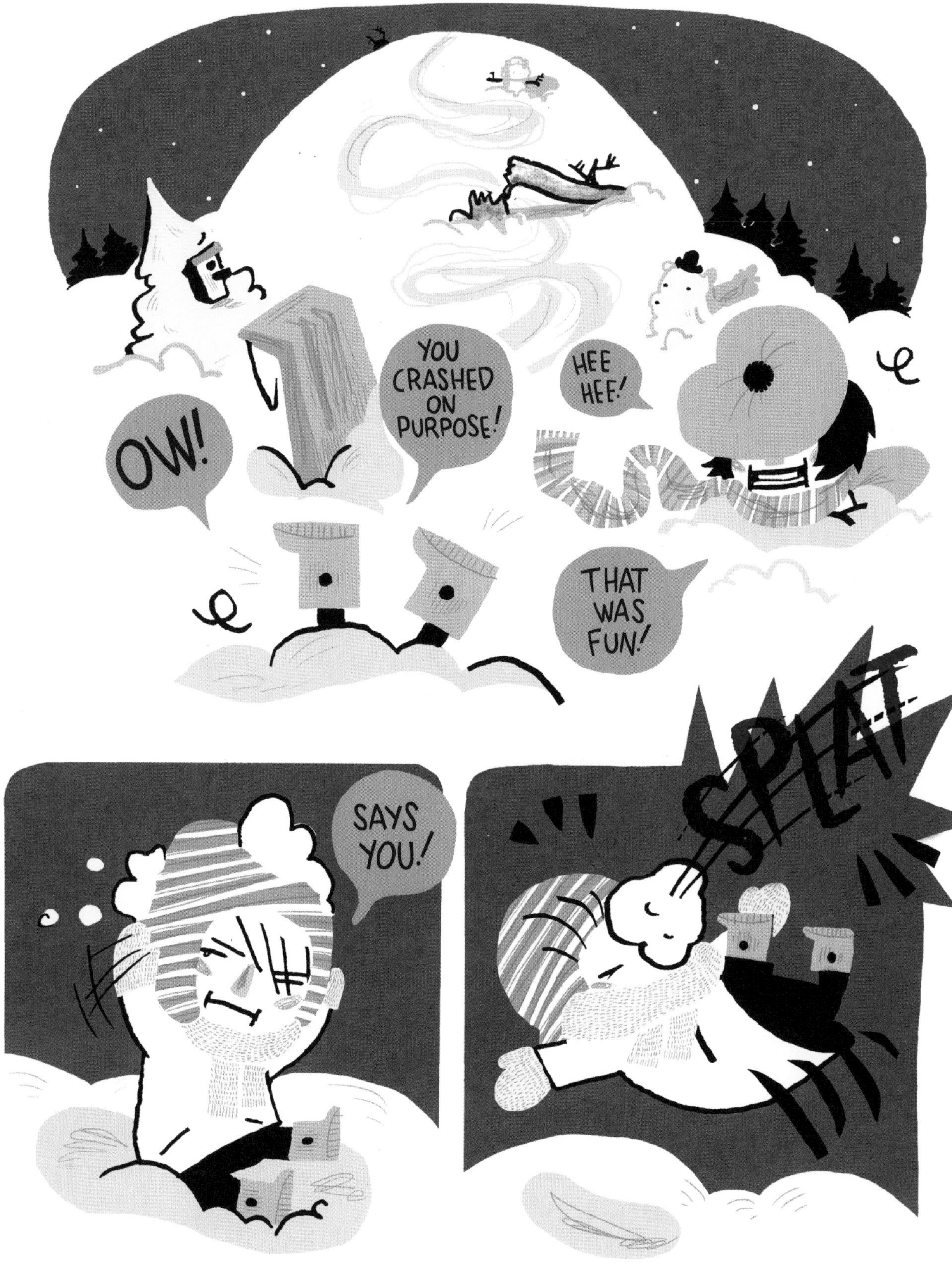
OW!
YOU CRASHED ON PURPOSE!
HEE HEE!
THAT WAS FUN!
SAYS YOU!
SPLAT

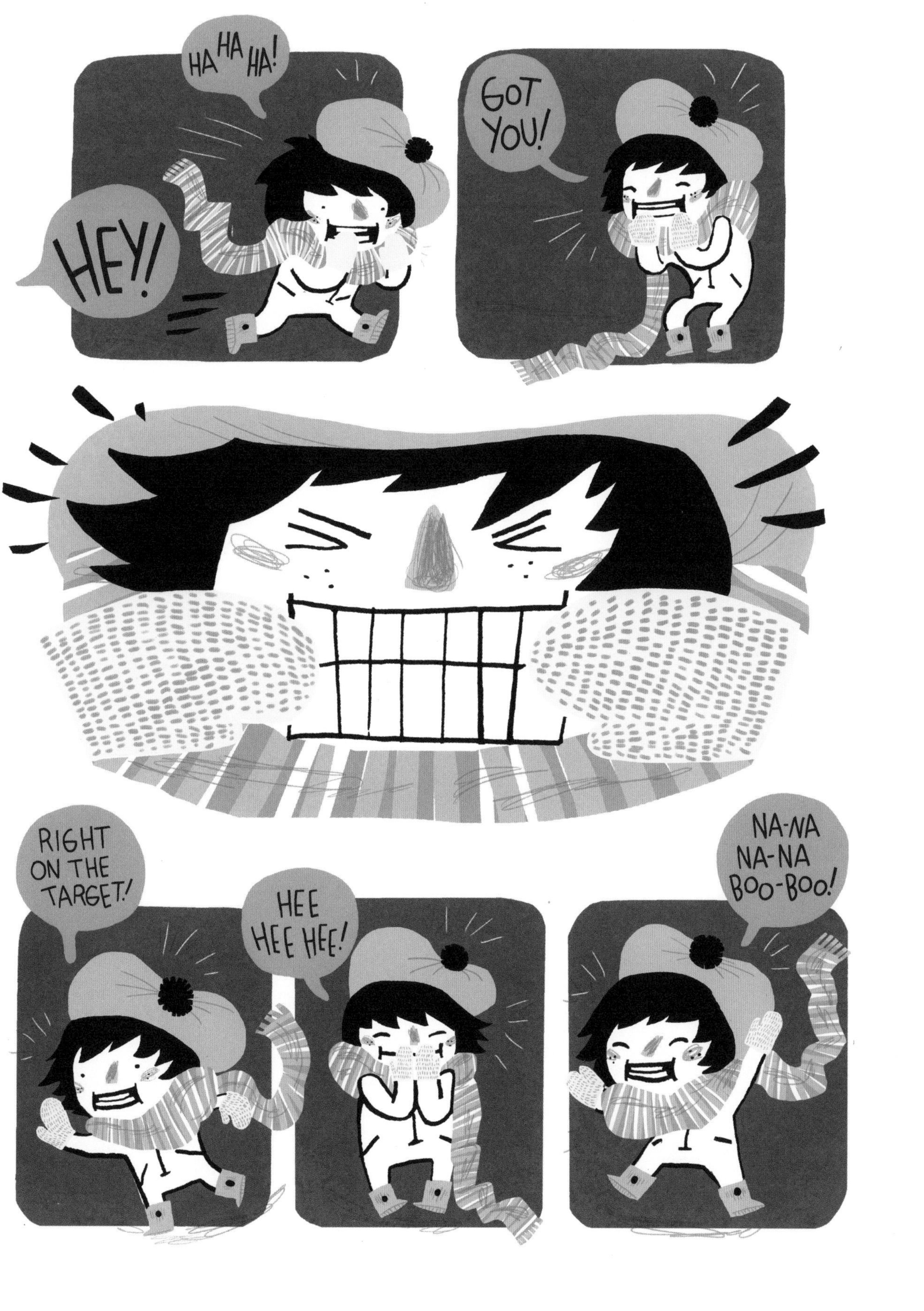
HA HA HA!
HEY!
GOT YOU!
RIGHT ON THE TARGET!
HEE HEE HEE!
NA-NA NA-NA BOO-BOO!

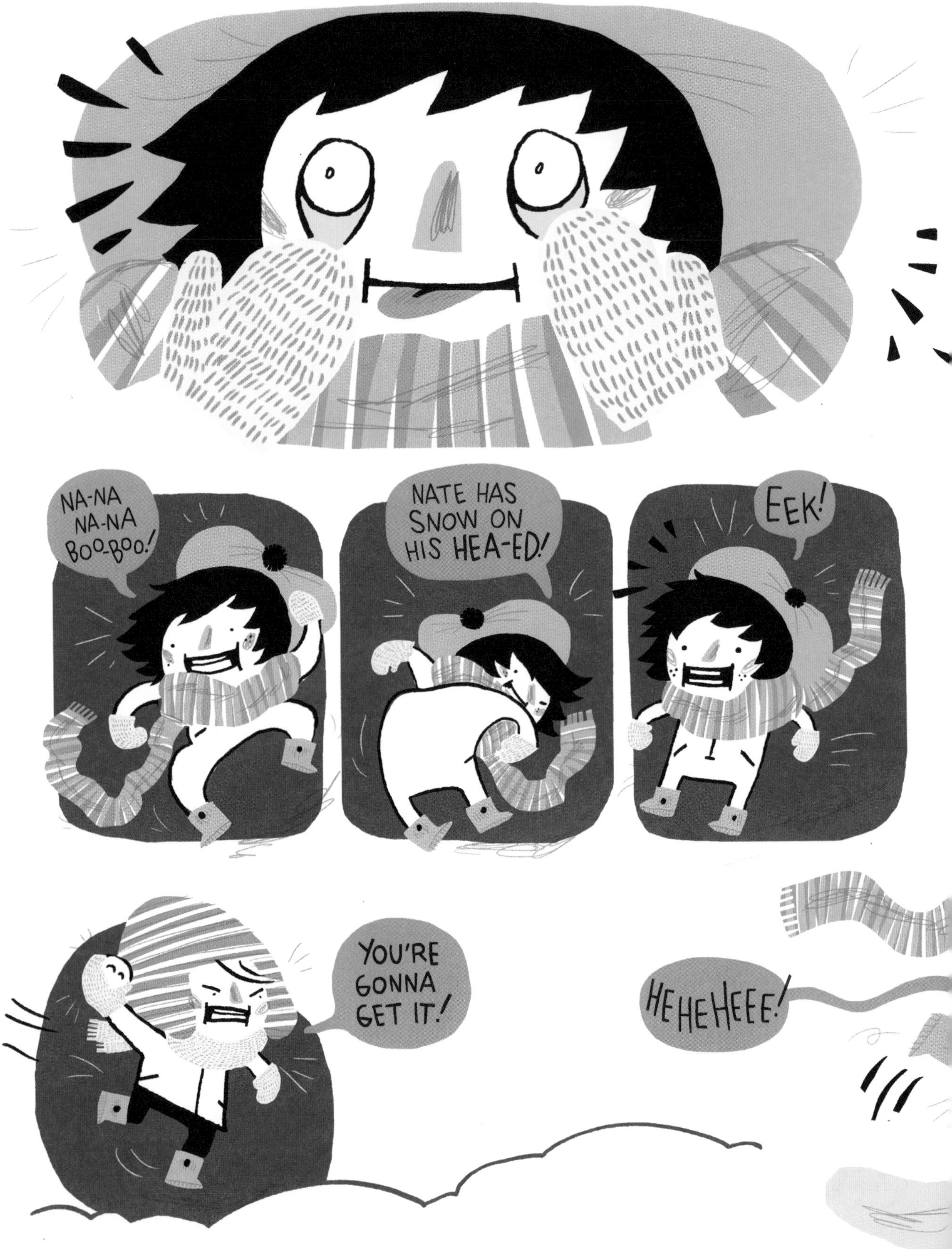
NA-NA NA-NA BOO-BOO!
NATE HAS SNOW ON HIS HEA-ED!
EEK!
YOU'RE GONNA GET IT!
HEHEHEEE!

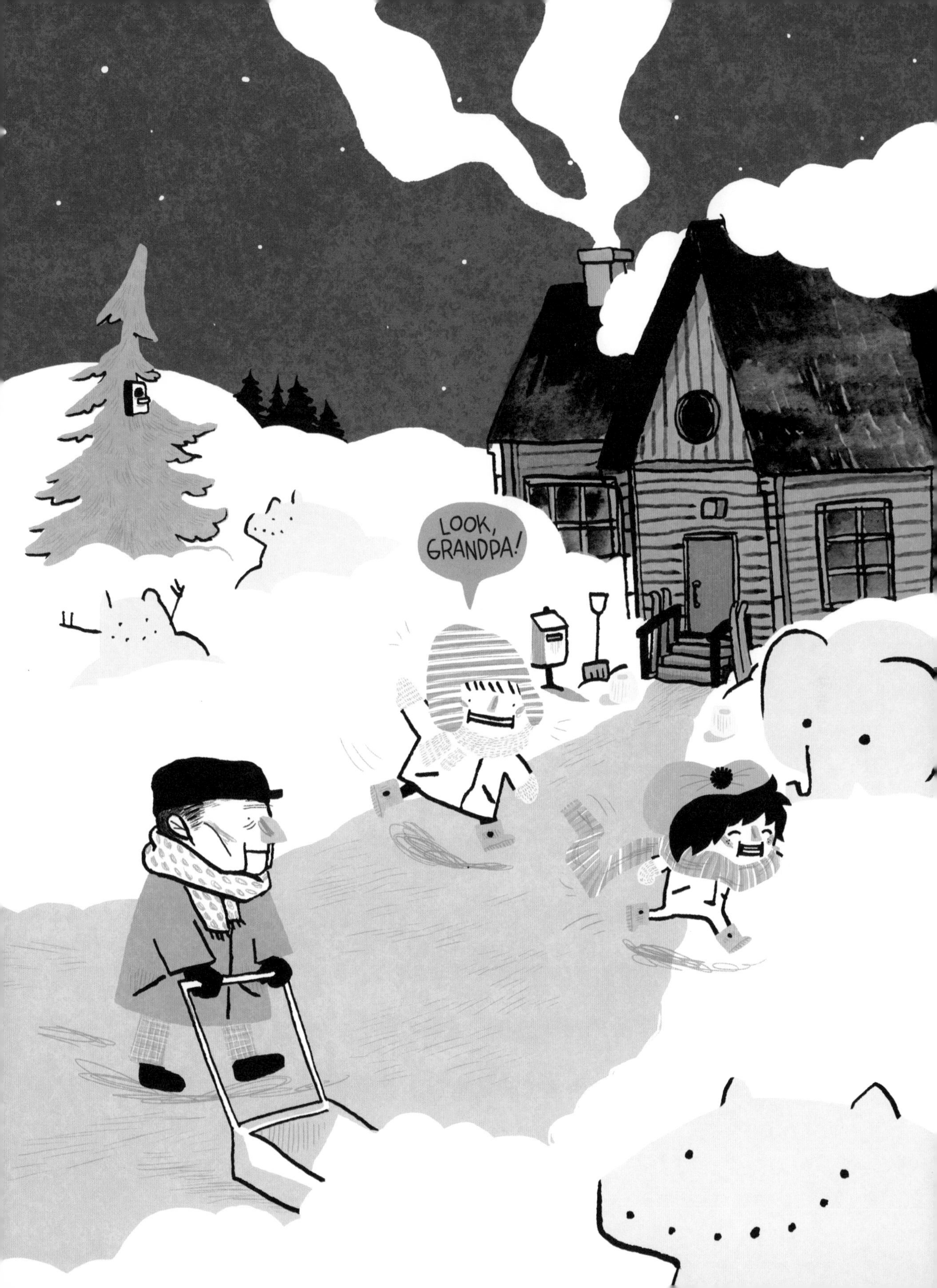
LOOK, GRANDPA!

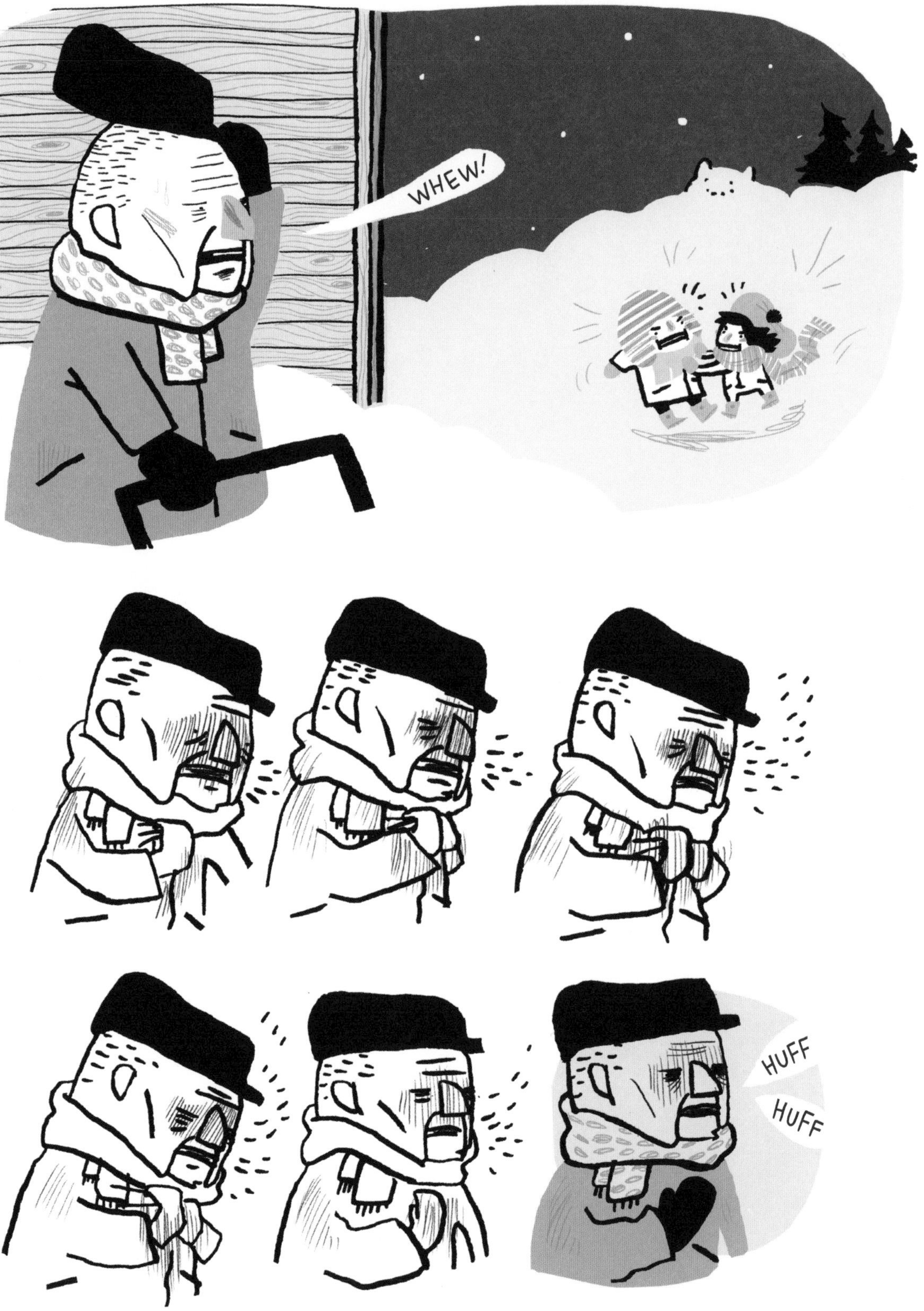
WHEW!
HUFF
HUFF

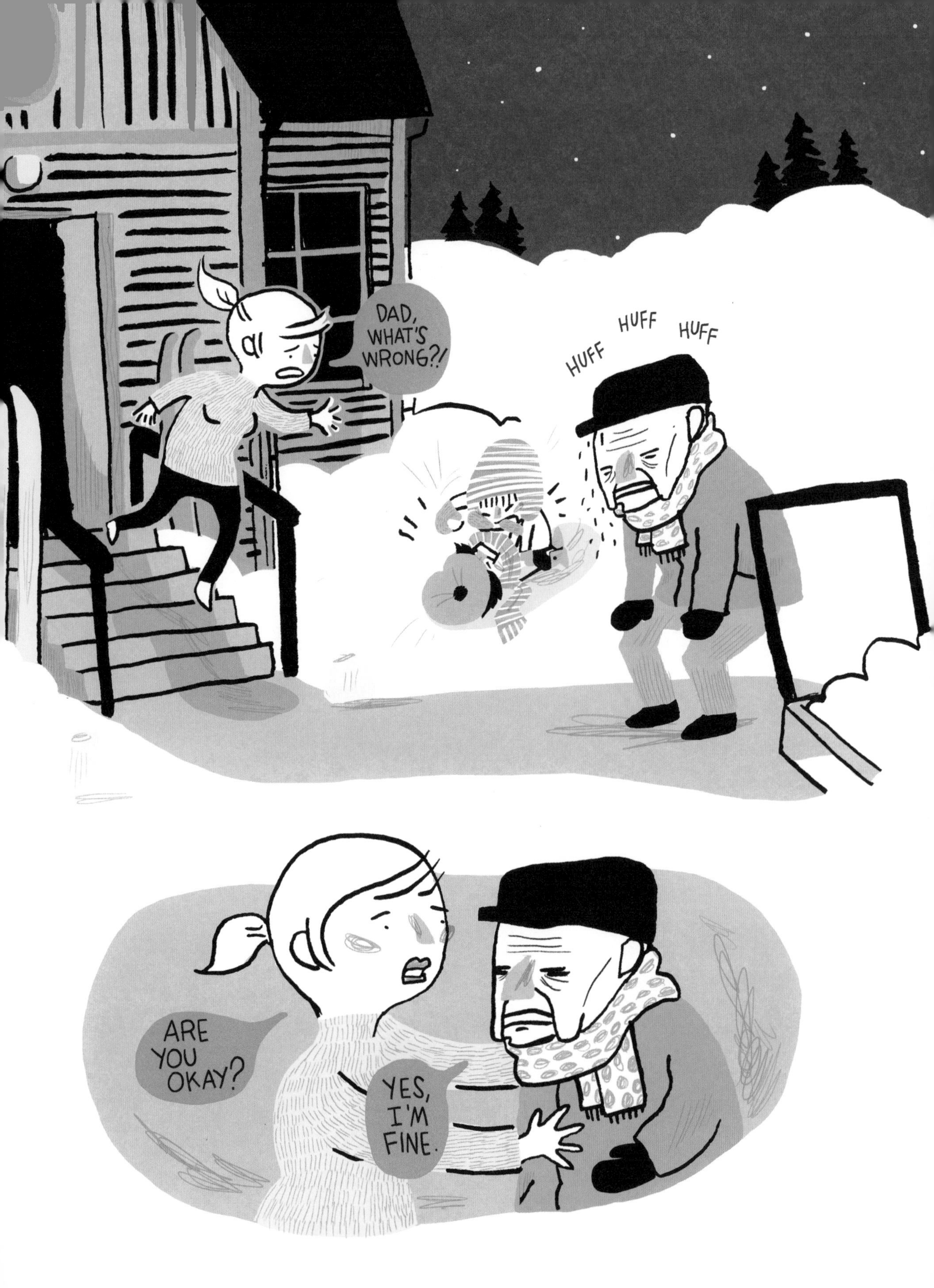
DAD, WHAT'S WRONG?!
HUFF HUFF HUFF HUFF
ARE YOU OKAY?
YES, I'M FINE.

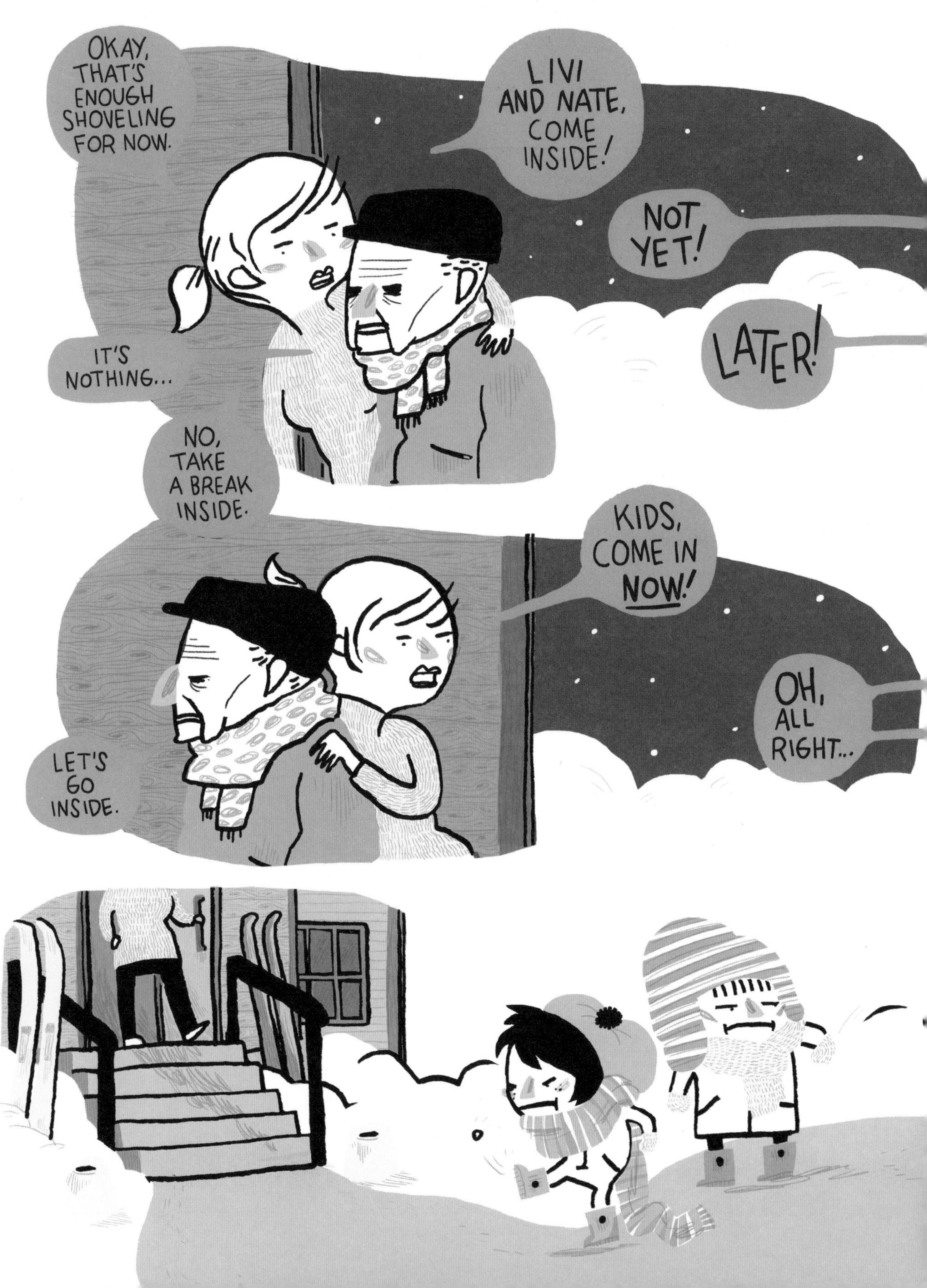
OKAY, THAT'S ENOUGH SHOVELING FOR NOW.
LIVI AND NATE, COME INSIDE!
NOT YET!
LATER!
IT'S NOTHING...
NO, TAKE A BREAK INSIDE.
KIDS, COME IN NOW!
OH, ALL RIGHT...
LET'S GO INSIDE.

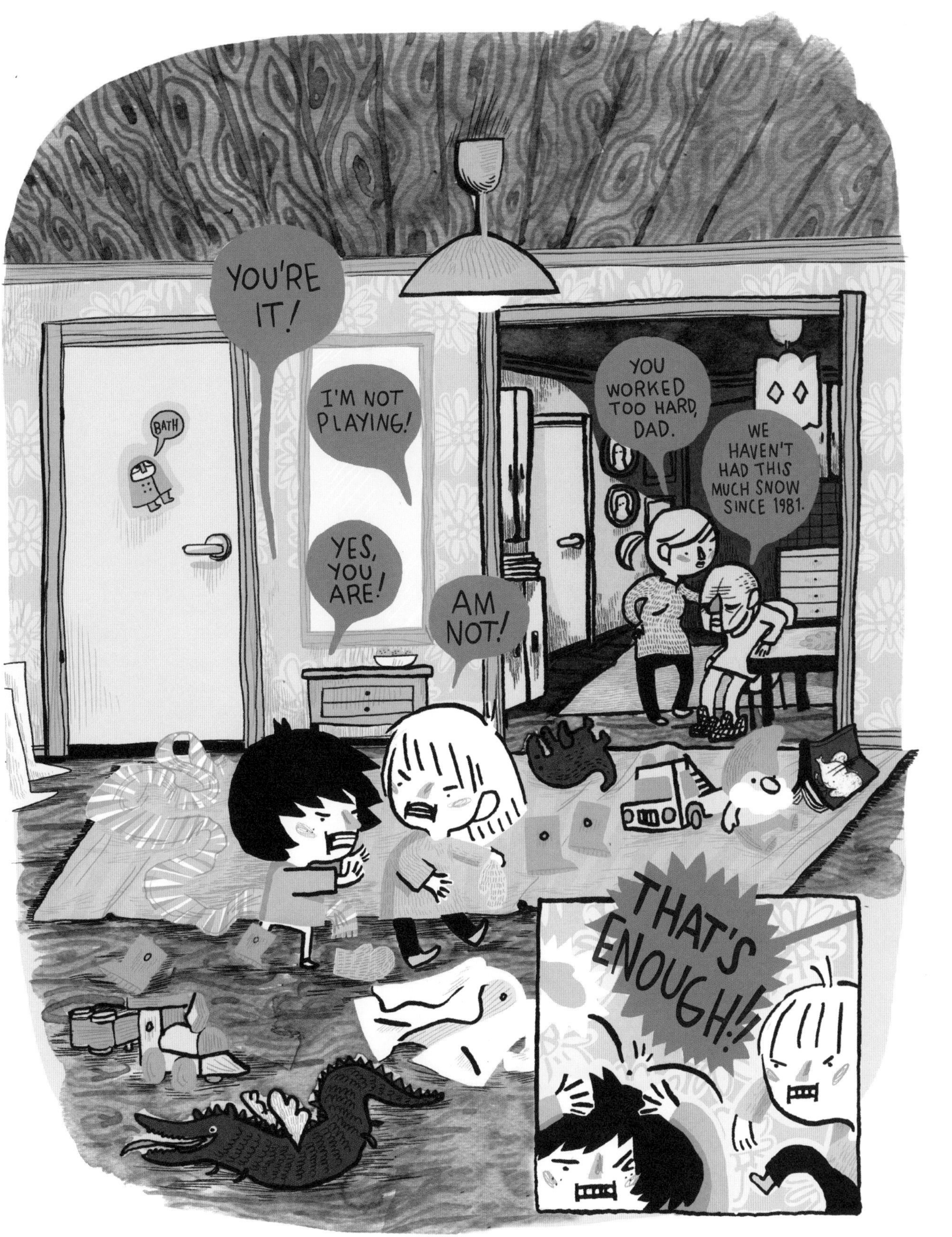
YOU'RE IT!
I'M NOT PLAYING!
YES, YOU ARE!
AM NOT!
BATH
YOU WORKED TOO HARD, DAD.
WE HAVEN'T HAD THIS MUCH SNOW SINCE 1981.
THAT'S ENOUGH!!

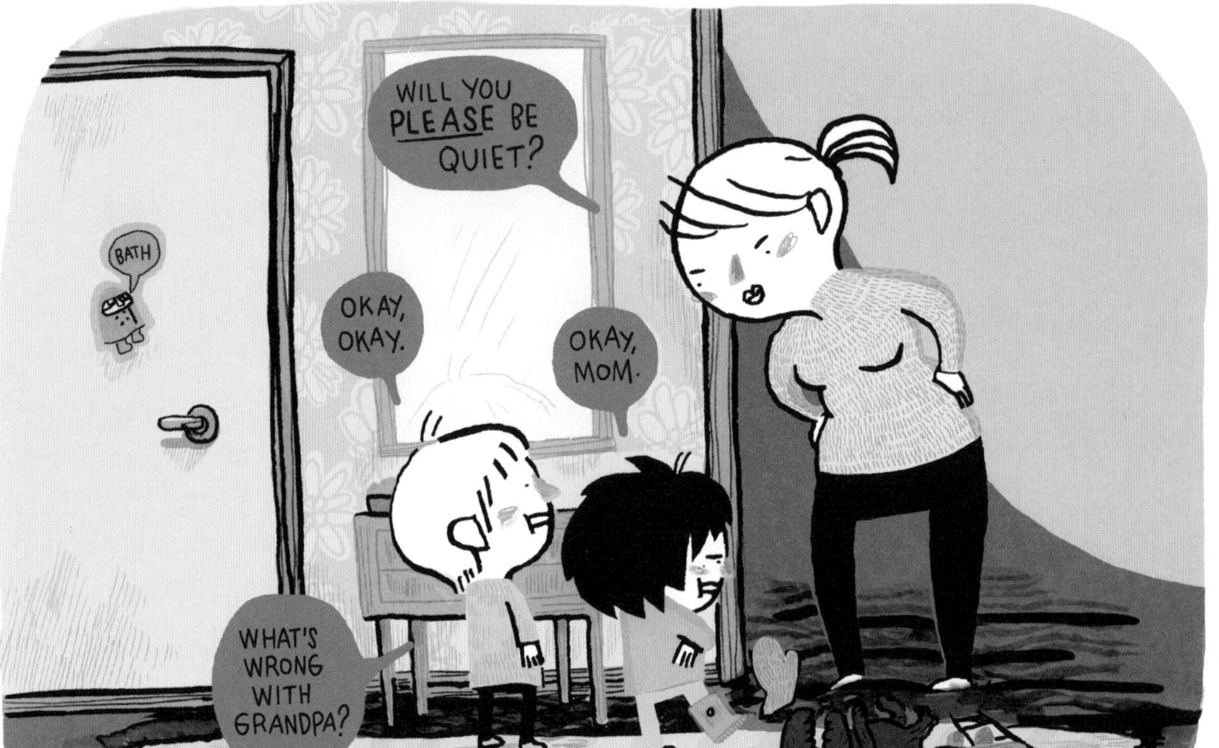
WILL YOU PLEASE BE QUIET?
BATH
OKAY, OKAY.
OKAY, MOM.
WHAT'S WRONG WITH GRANDPA?

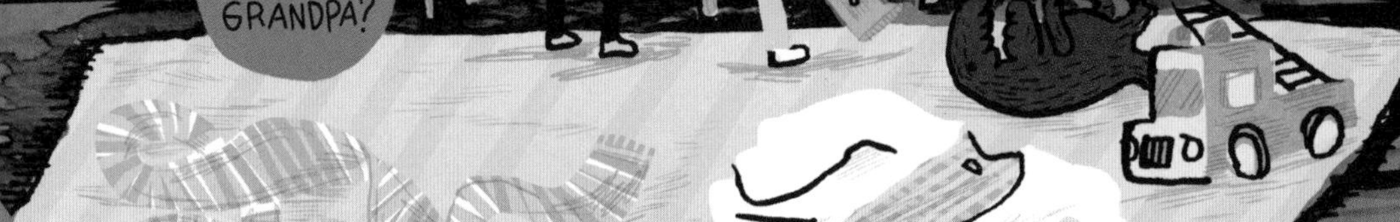
IS GRANDPA DYING?
NO, HE'S JUST A LITTLE TIRED.

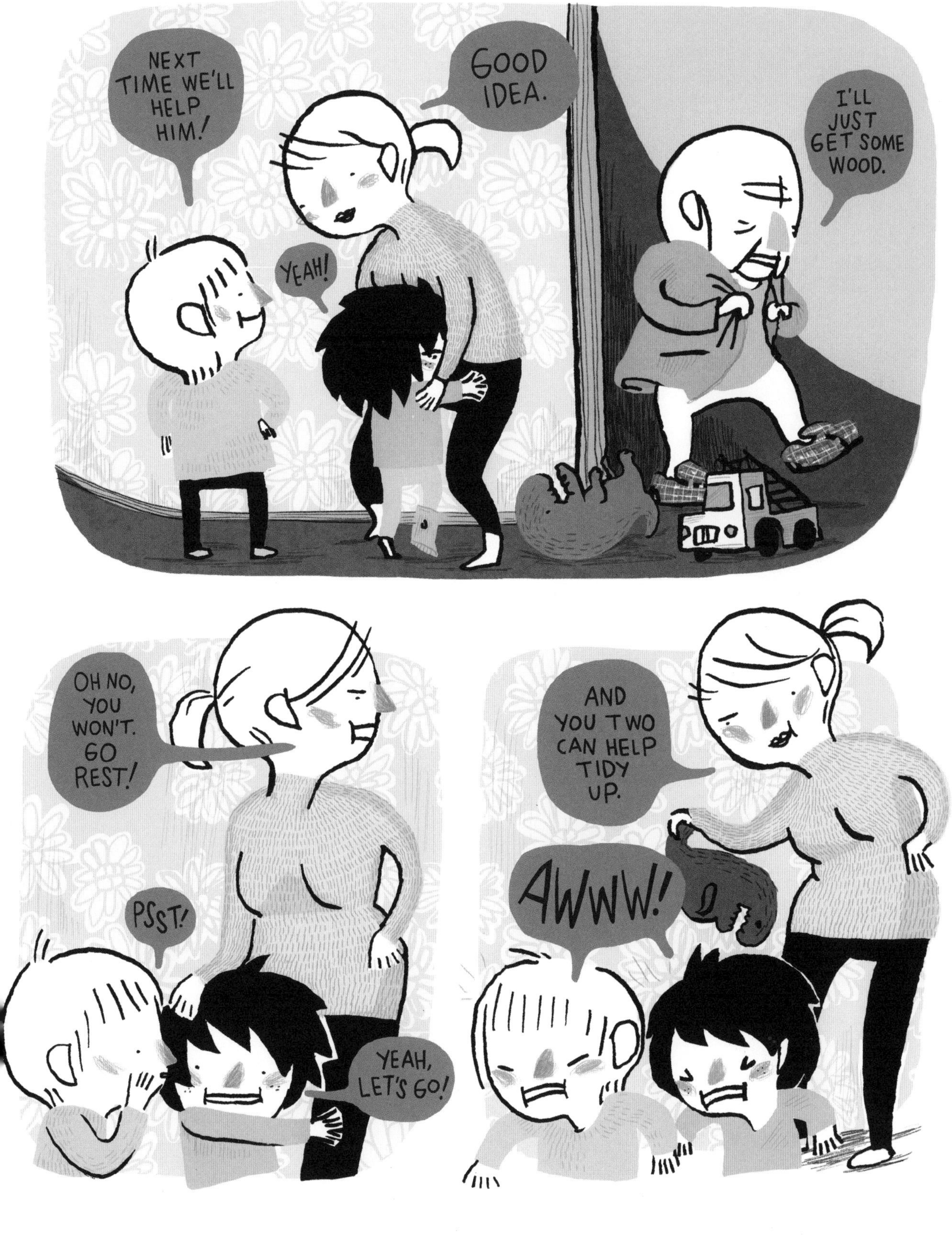
NEXT TIME WE'LL HELP HIM!
GOOD IDEA.
YEAH!
I'LL JUST GET SOME WOOD.
OH NO, YOU WON'T. GO REST!
PSST!
YEAH, LET'S GO!
AND YOU TWO CAN HELP TIDY UP.
AWWW!

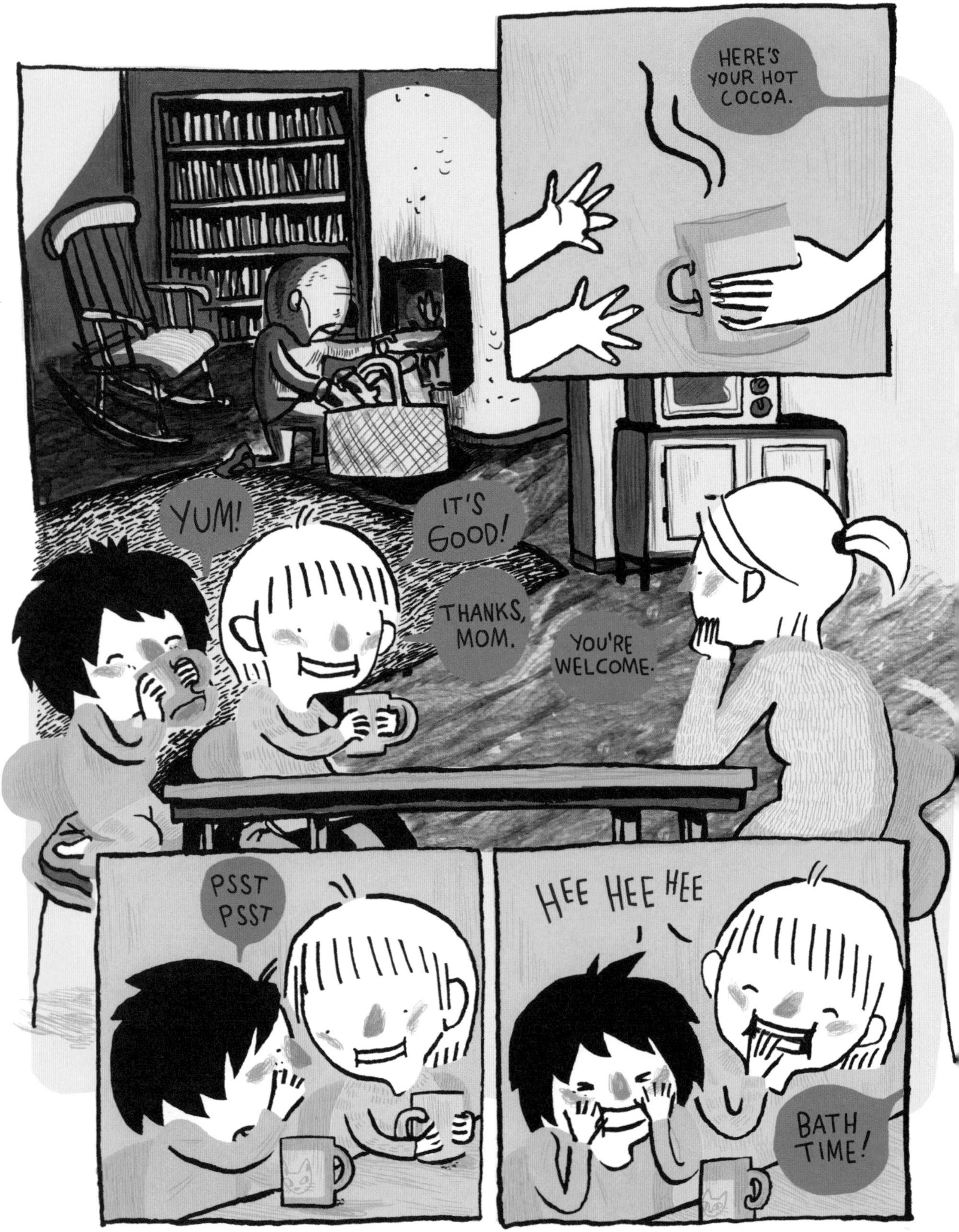
HERE'S YOUR HOT COCOA.
YUM!
IT'S GOOD!
THANKS, MOM.
YOU'RE WELCOME.
PSST PSST
HEE HEE HEE
BATH TIME!

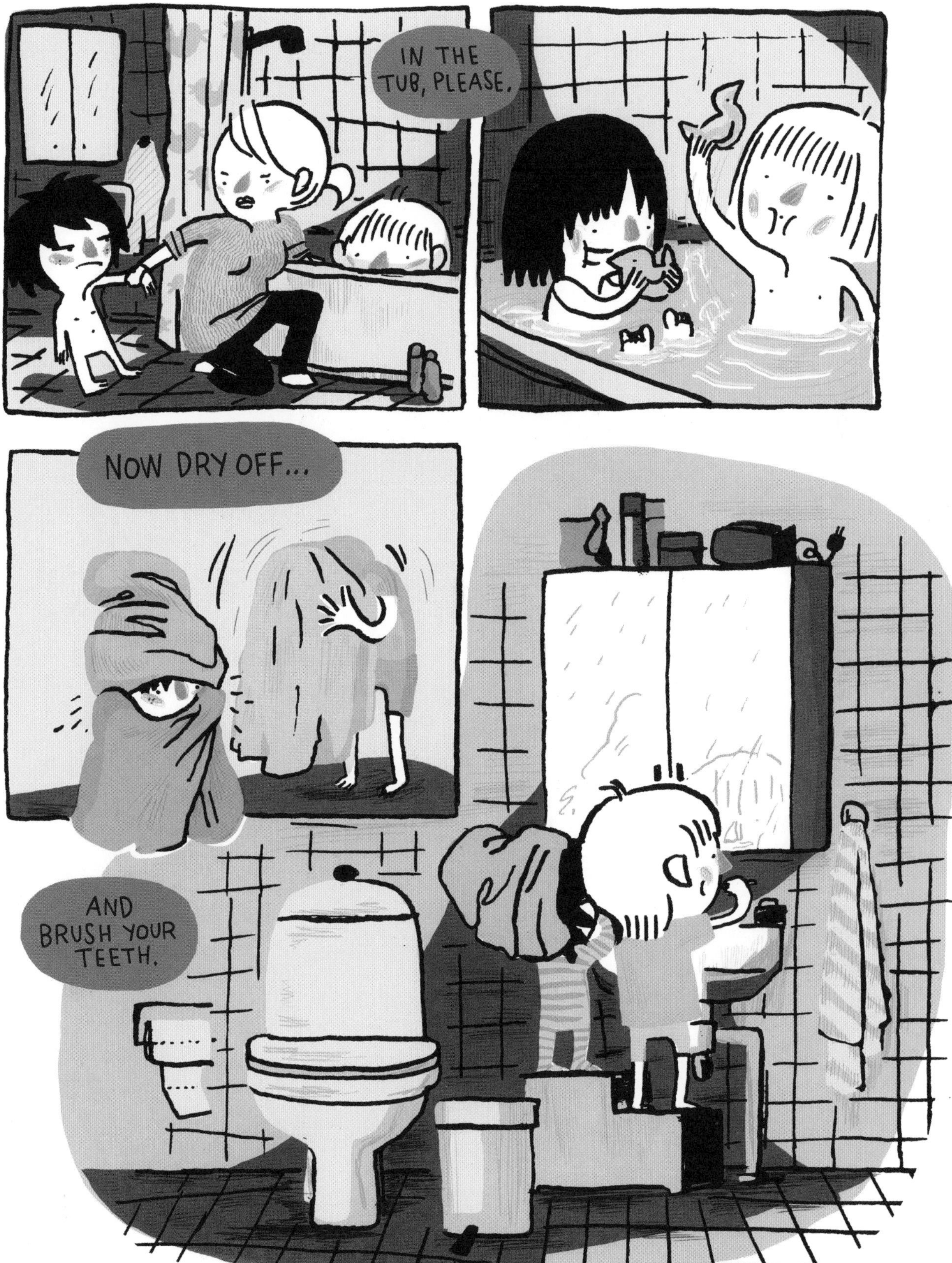
IN THE TUB, PLEASE.
NOW DRY OFF...
AND BRUSH YOUR TEETH.

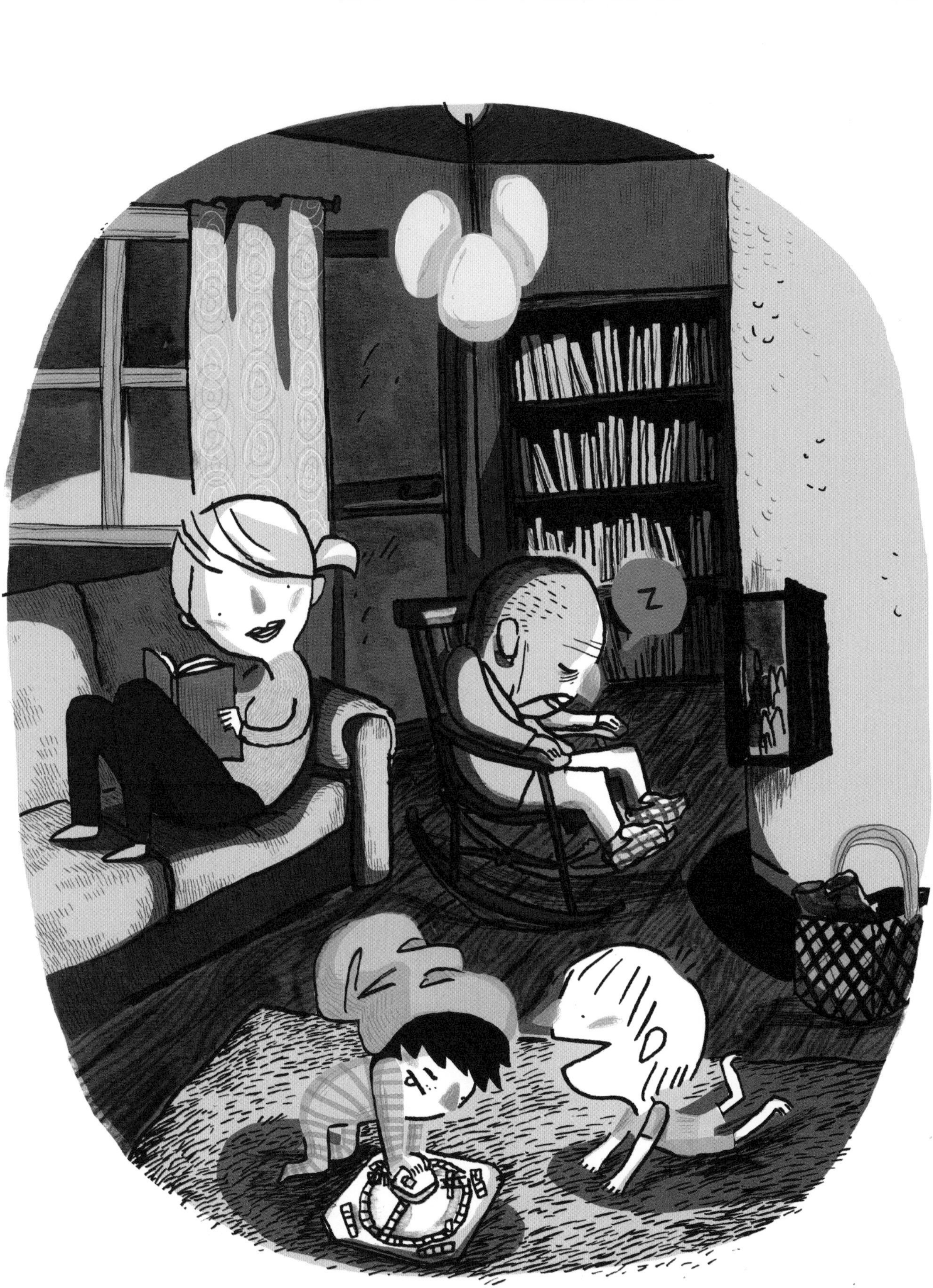
z

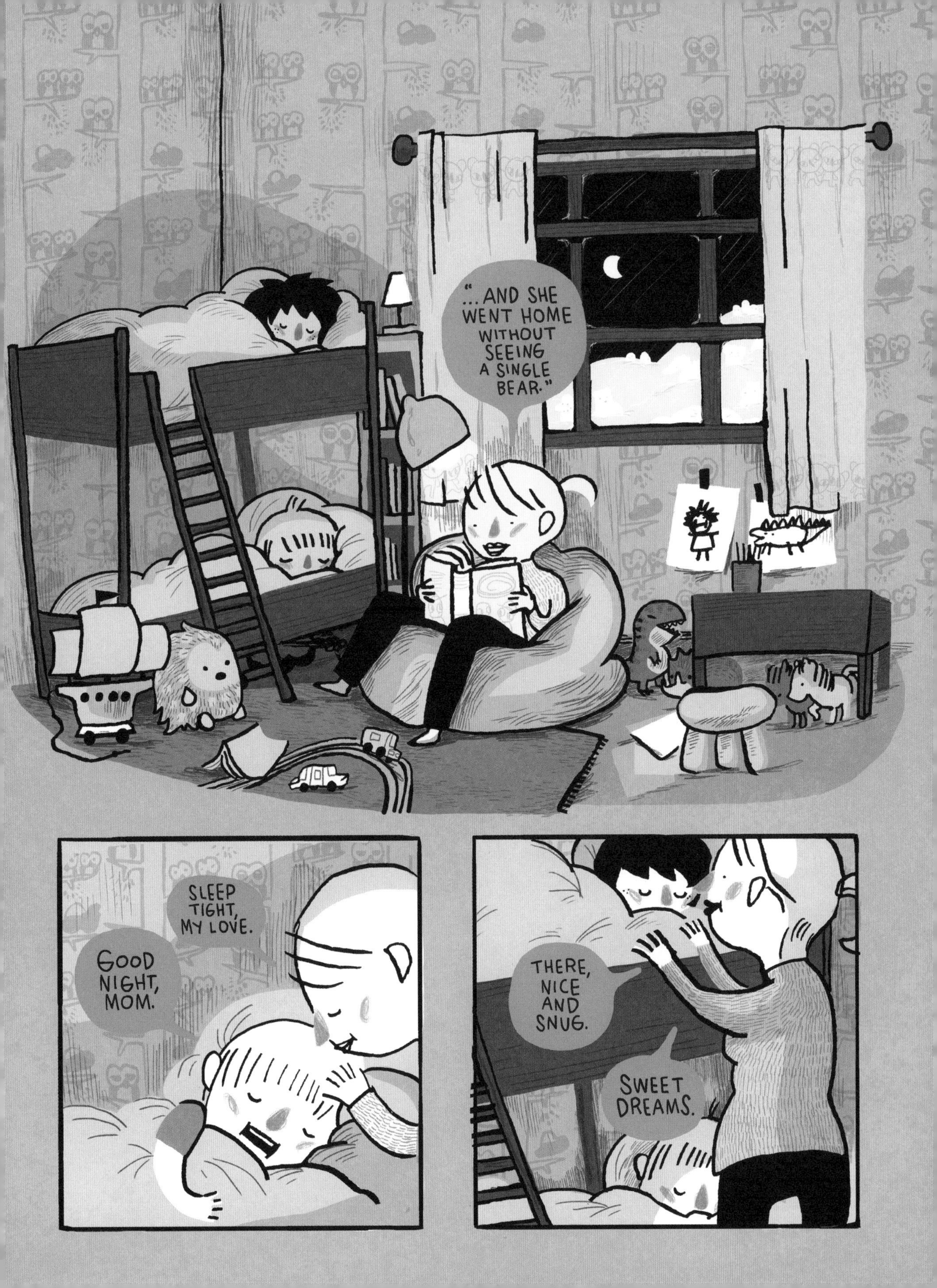
"...AND SHE WENT HOME WITHOUT SEEING A SINGLE BEAR."
SLEEP TIGHT, MY LOVE.
GOOD NIGHT, MOM.
THERE, NICE AND SNUG.
SWEET DREAMS.

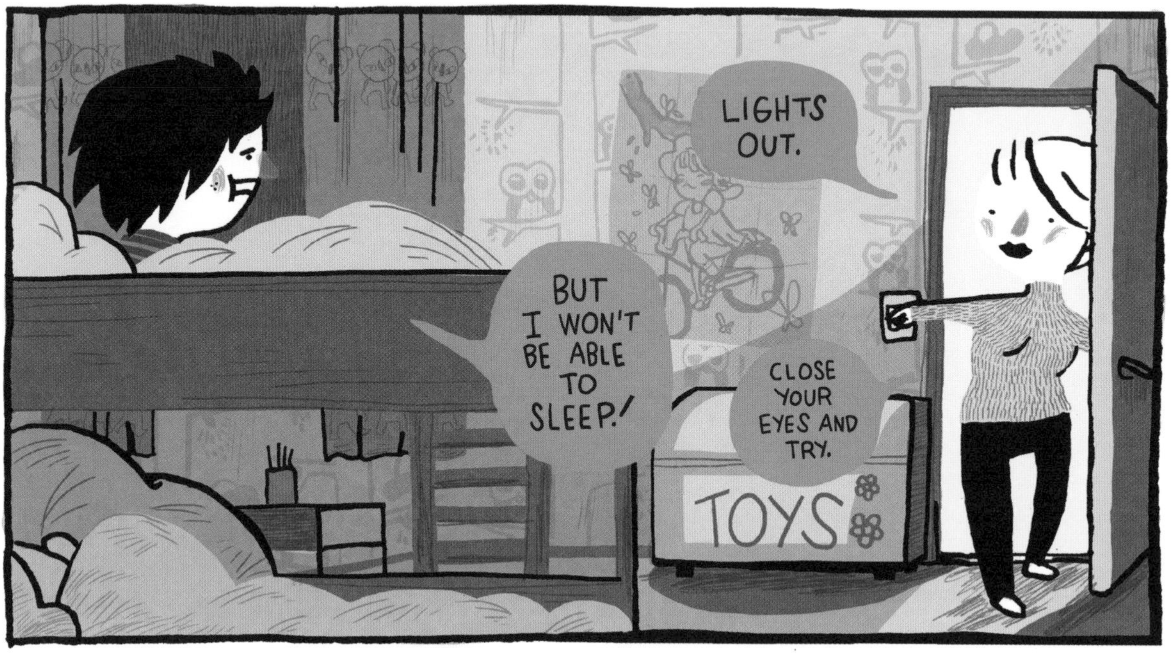
LIGHTS OUT.
BUT I WON'T BE ABLE TO SLEEP!
CLOSE YOUR EYES AND TRY.
TOYS

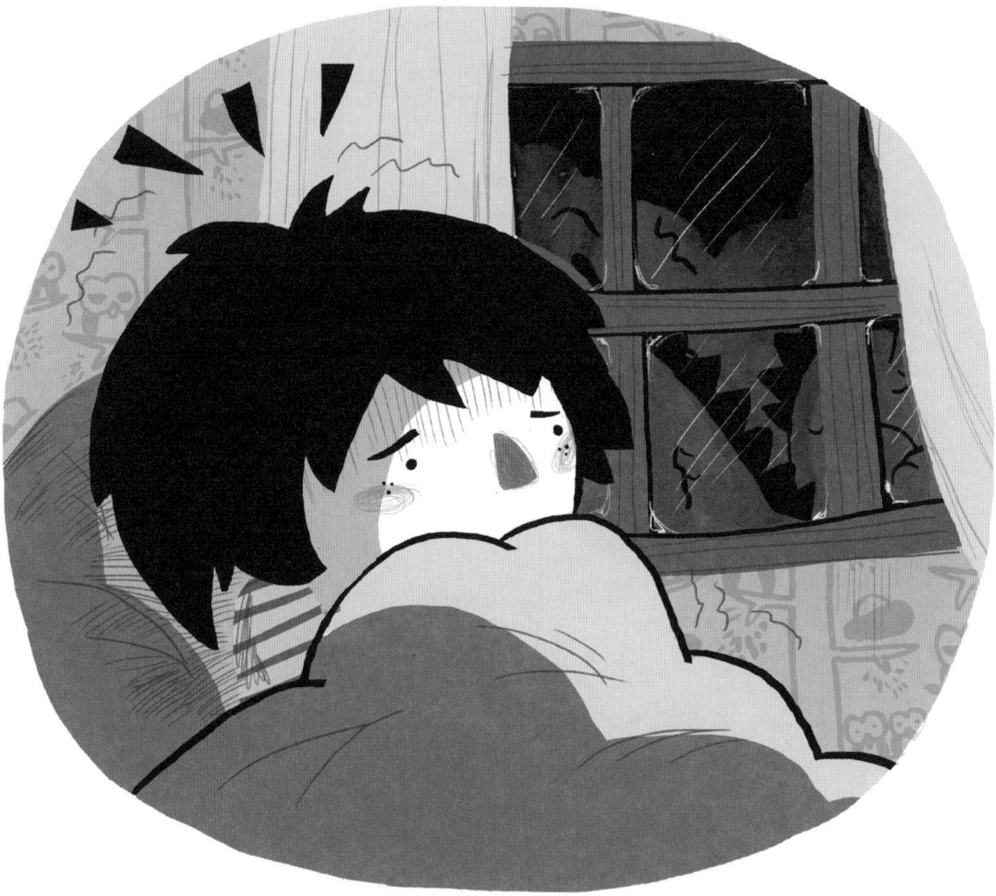

PSST...
PSST!
NATE!
ARE YOU ASLEEP?
NOT YET.
DID YOU SEE SOMETHING MOVE OUTSIDE?
NO, NOTHING.
IT WAS A DRAGON!!
NO, IT WAS JUST A DREAM.
MOMMY!!
WHAT'S WRONG?
SOMETHING'S MOVING OUTSIDE!
LIVI'S AFRAID OF OUR SNOW ANIMALS.
TOYS

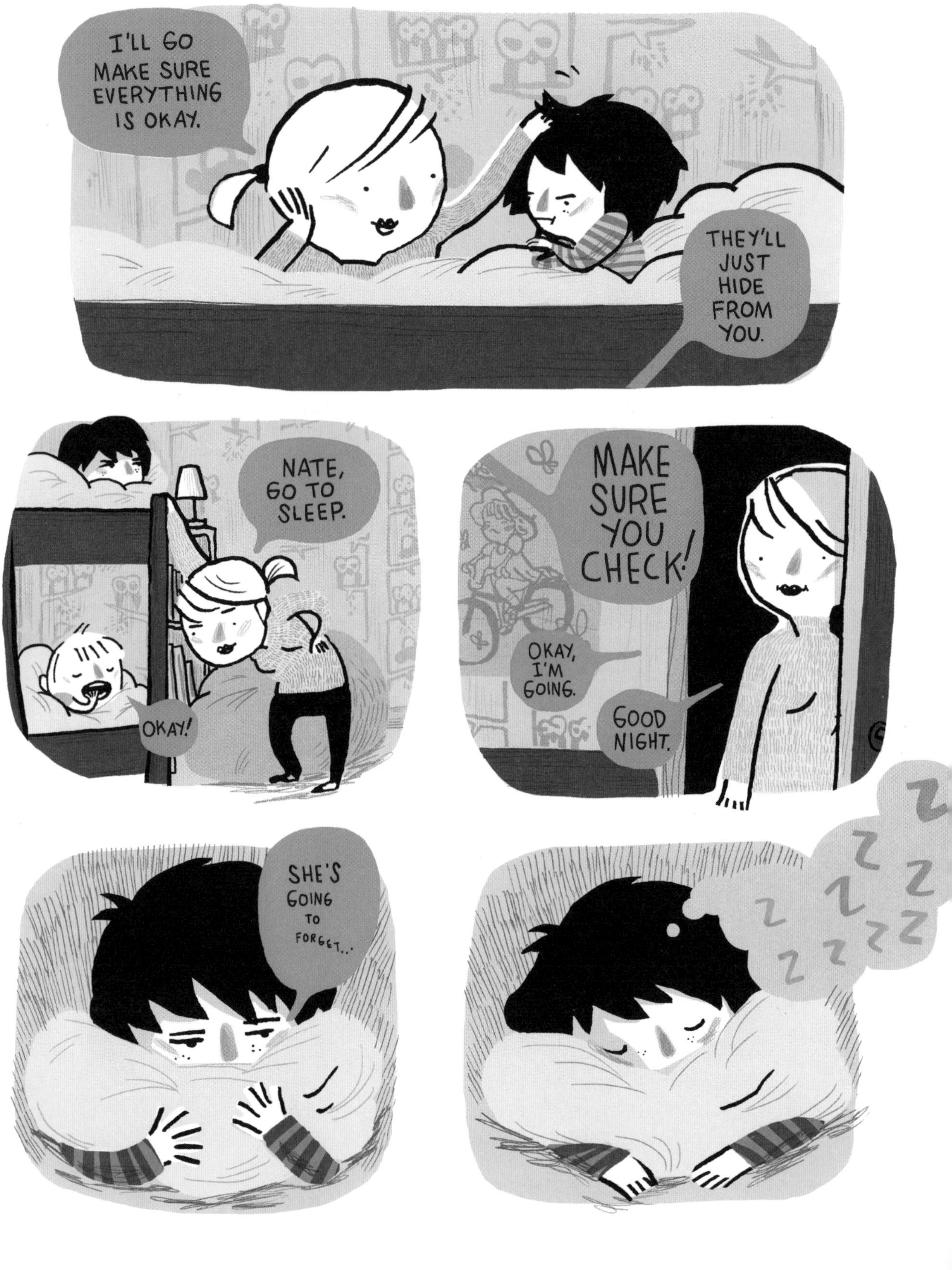
I'LL GO MAKE SURE EVERYTHING IS OKAY.
THEY'LL JUST HIDE FROM YOU.
NATE, GO TO SLEEP.
OKAY!
MAKE SURE YOU CHECK!
OKAY, I'M GOING.
GOOD NIGHT.
SHE'S GOING TO FORGET...

ZZZZZZZZZ
LIVI'S TEA PARTY
KNOCK KNOCK
THESE CAKES ARE SO DELICIOUS!
AND THE TEA IS LOVELY.
NOM NOM
WHO COULD BE KNOCKING?

KNOCK KNOCK
WE WEREN'T EXPECTING ANY GUESTS.
WHO IS IT?

WHAT IF IT'S A ROBBER?
WE DON'T HAVE TO OPEN IT.

BUT...
OKAY, LET'S OPEN IT.

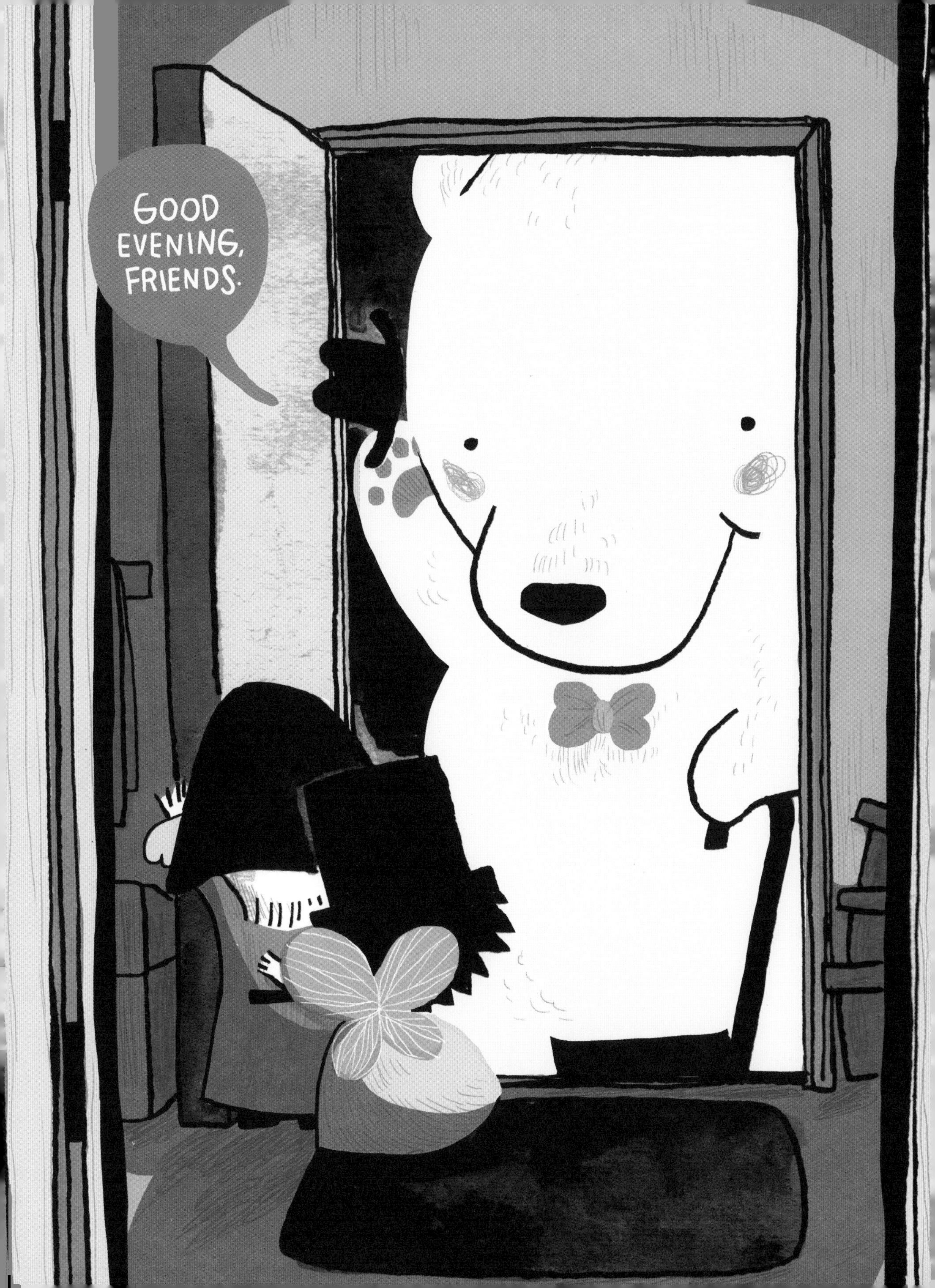
GOOD EVENING, FRIENDS.

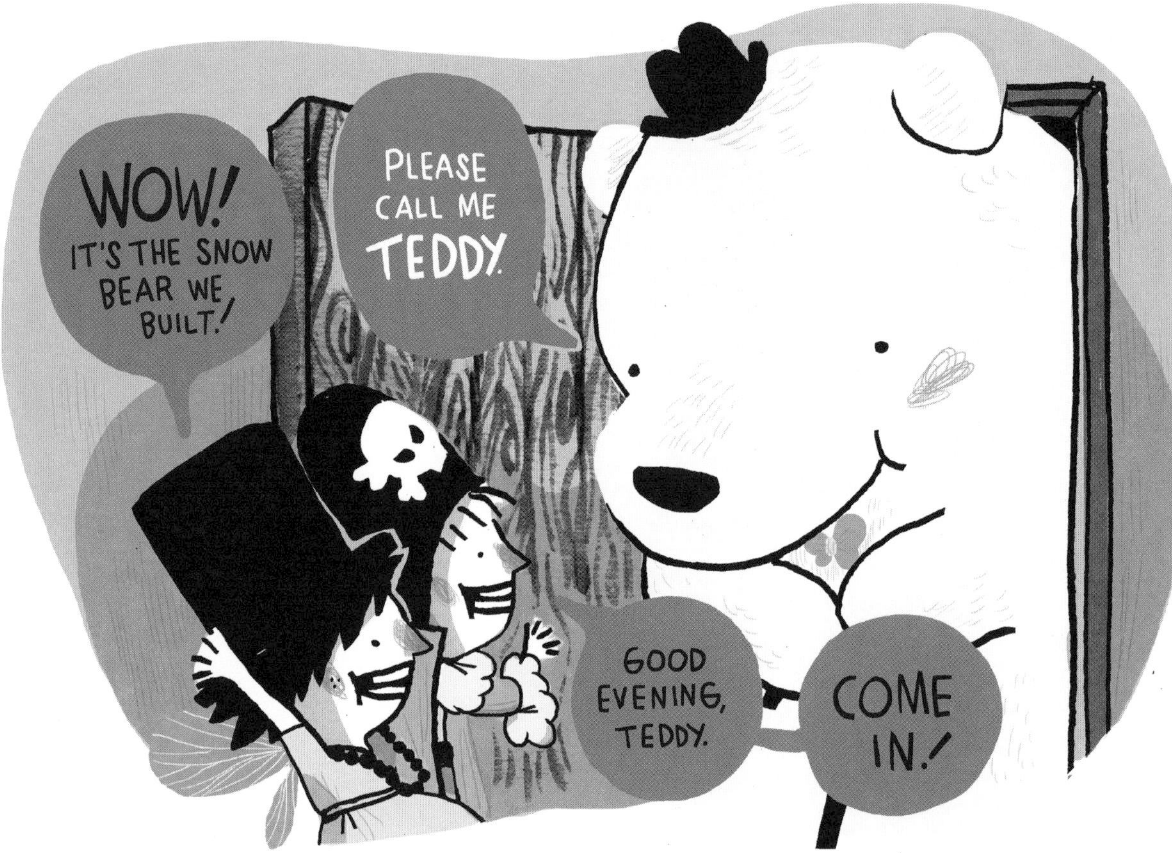
WOW! IT'S THE SNOW BEAR WE BUILT!
PLEASE CALL ME TEDDY.
GOOD EVENING, TEDDY.
COME IN!

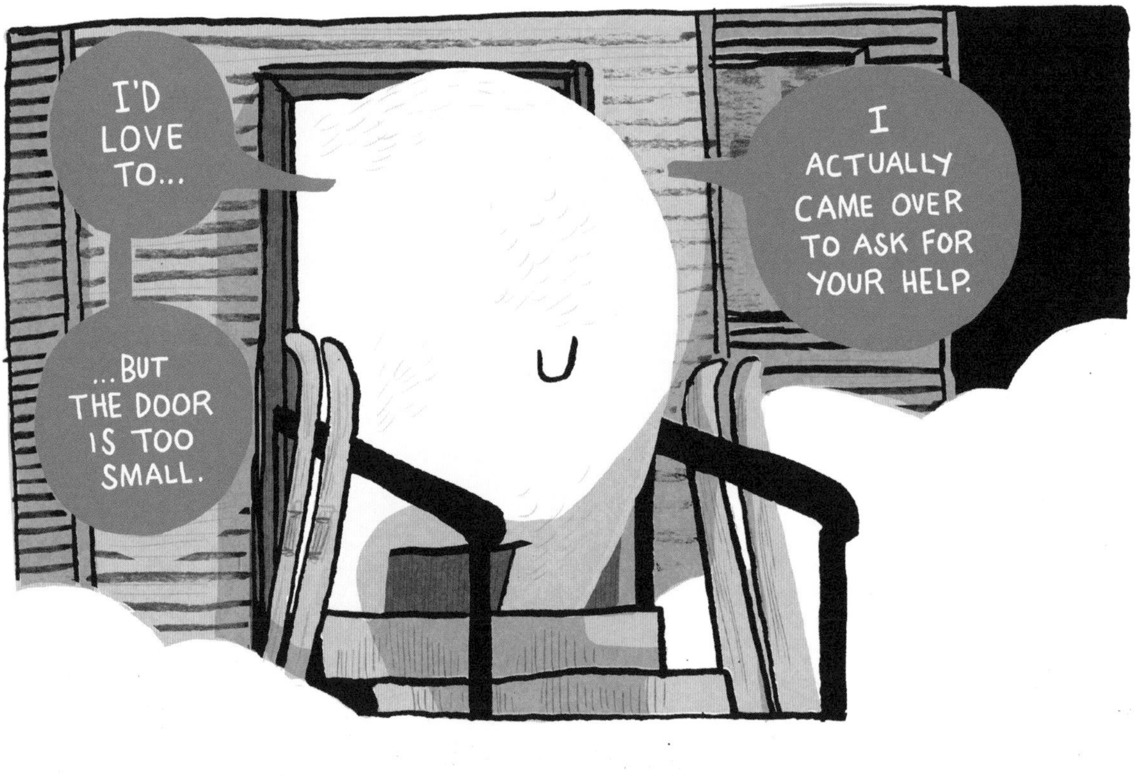
I'D LOVE TO...
...BUT THE DOOR IS TOO SMALL.
I ACTUALLY CAME OVER TO ASK FOR YOUR HELP.

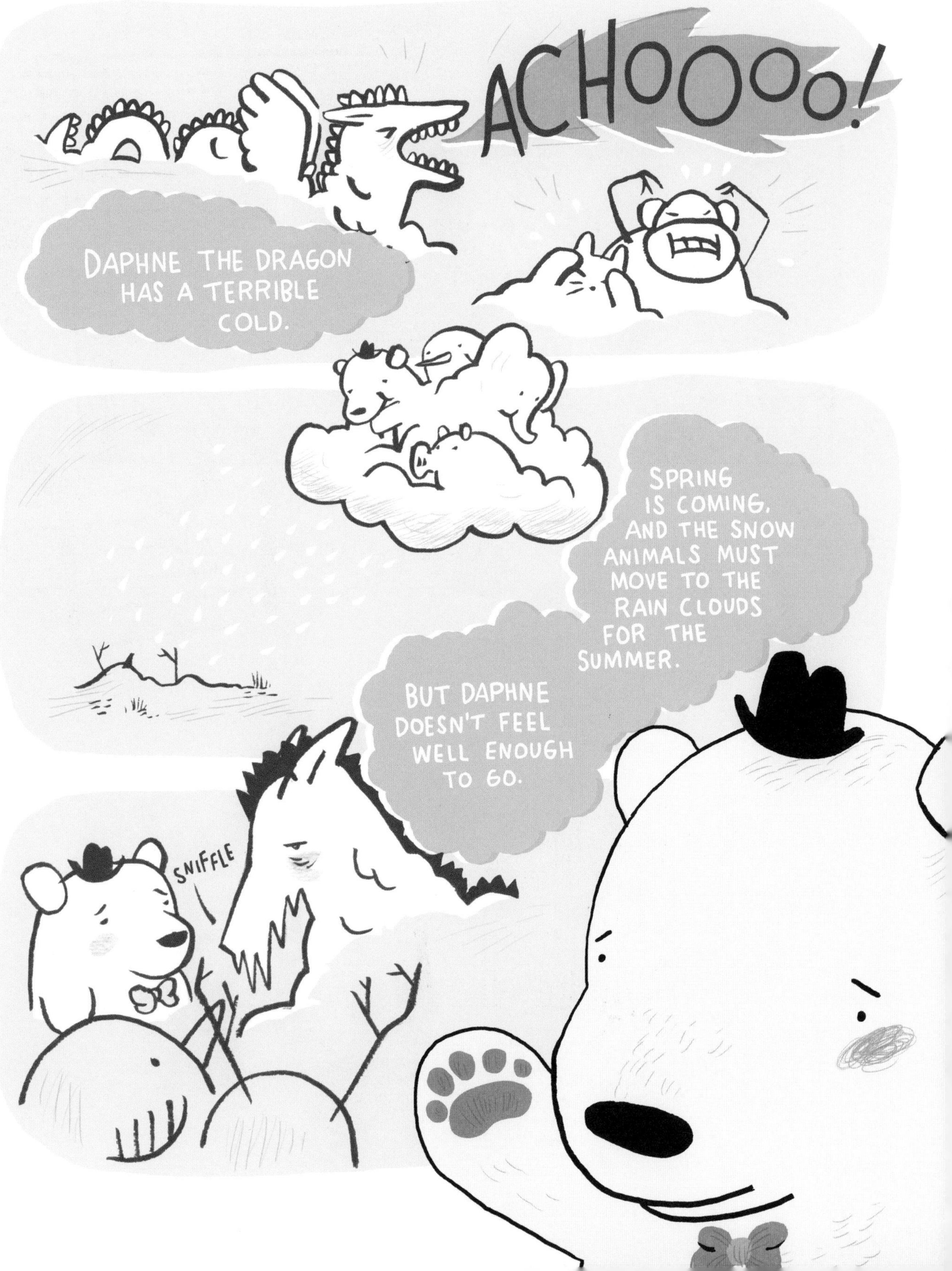

ACHOOOoo!
DAPHNE THE DRAGON HAS A TERRIBLE COLD.
SPRING IS COMING, AND THE SNOW ANIMALS MUST MOVE TO THE RAIN CLOUDS FOR THE SUMMER.
BUT DAPHNE DOESN'T FEEL WELL ENOUGH TO GO.
SNIFFLE

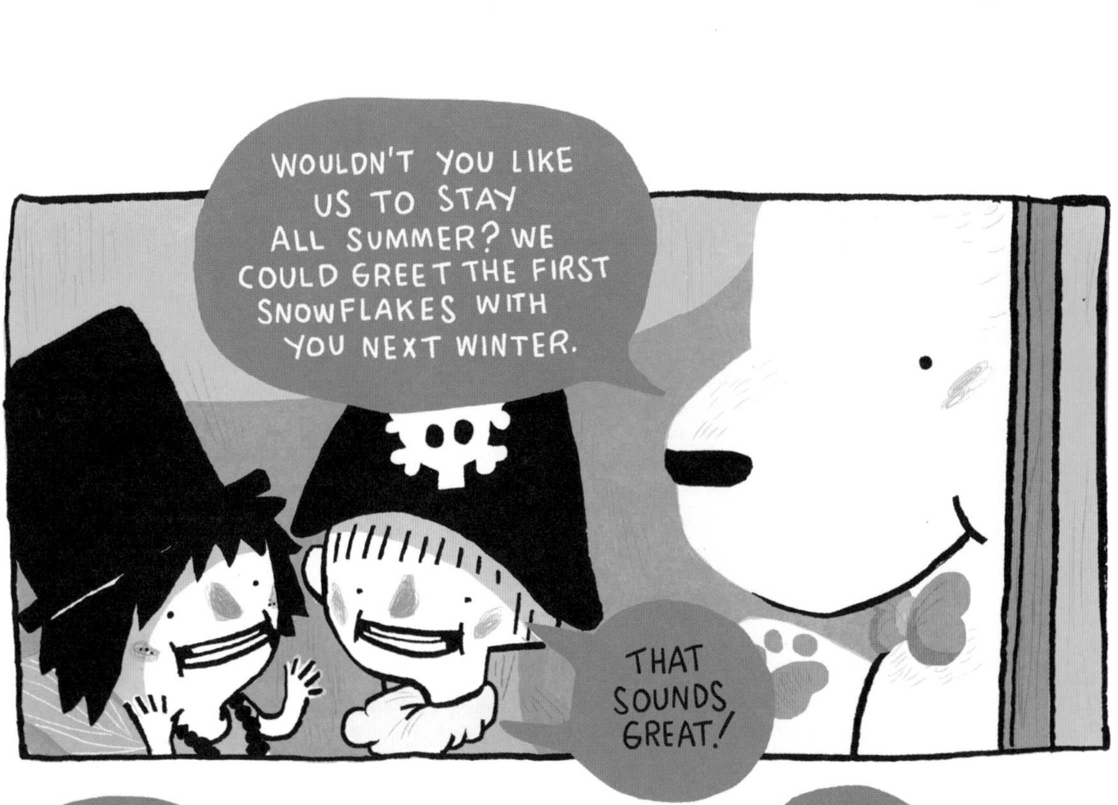
WOULDN'T YOU LIKE US TO STAY ALL SUMMER? WE COULD GREET THE FIRST SNOWFLAKES WITH YOU NEXT WINTER.
THAT SOUNDS GREAT!

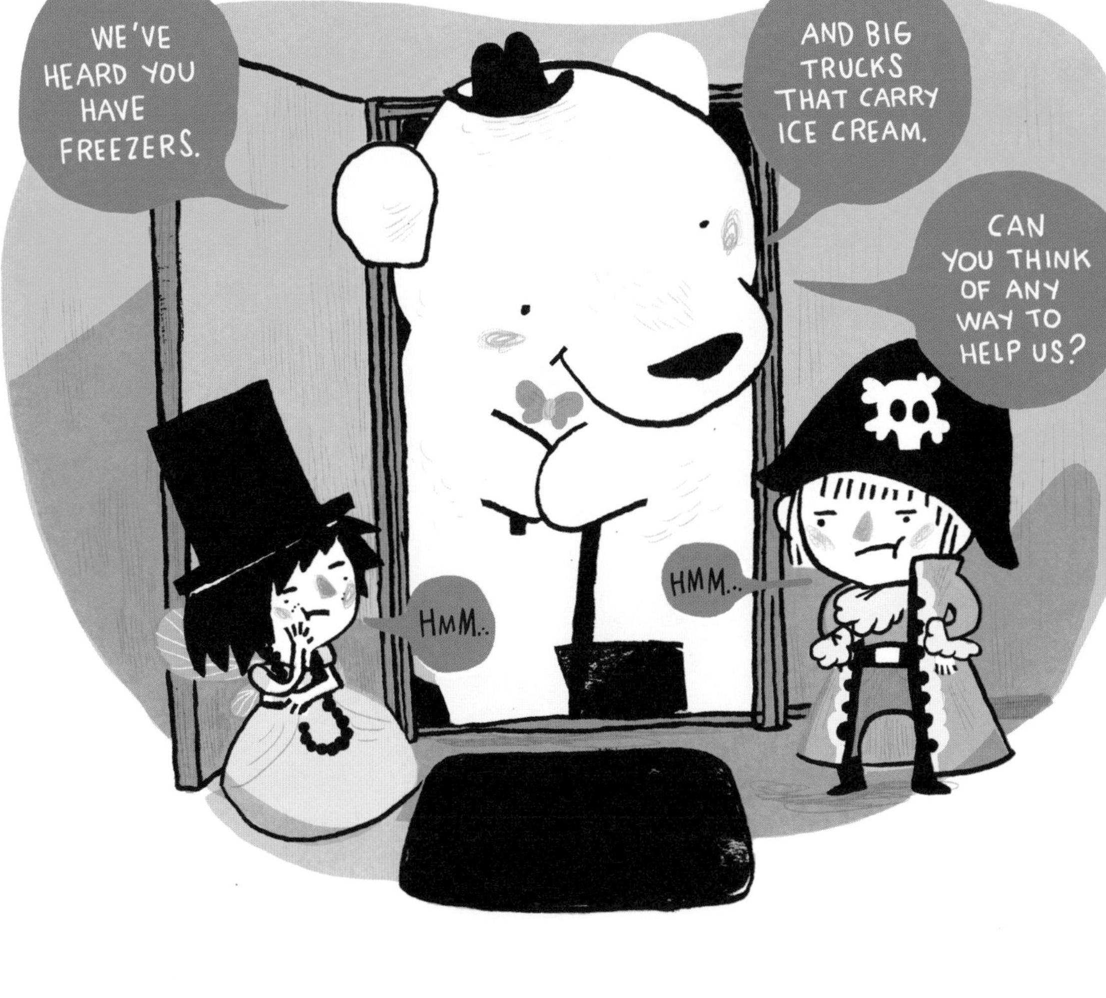
WE'VE HEARD YOU HAVE FREEZERS.
AND BIG TRUCKS THAT CARRY ICE CREAM.
CAN YOU THINK OF ANY WAY TO HELP US?
HMM..
HMM..

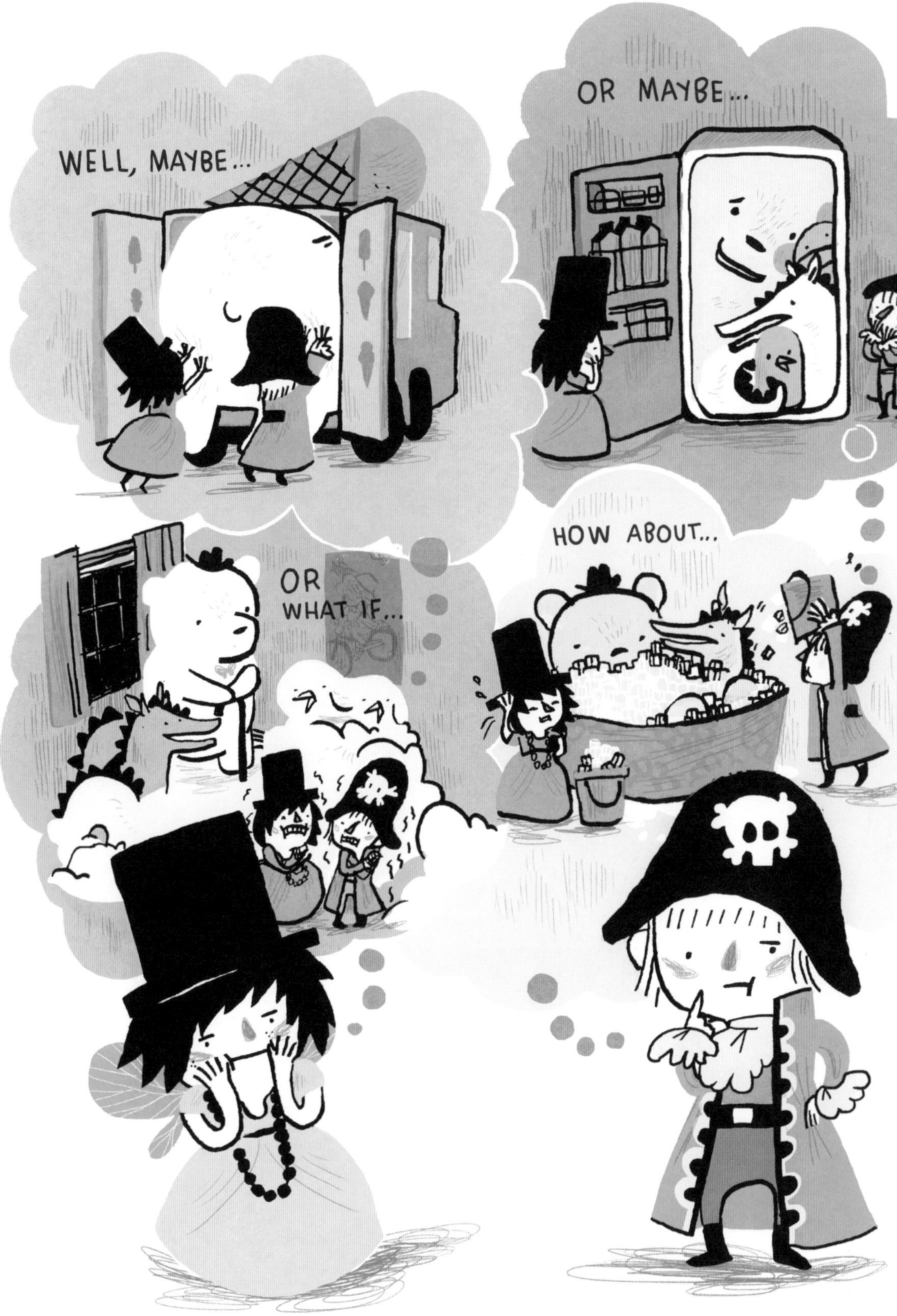

WELL, MAYBE...
OR MAYBE...
OR WHAT IF...
HOW ABOUT...

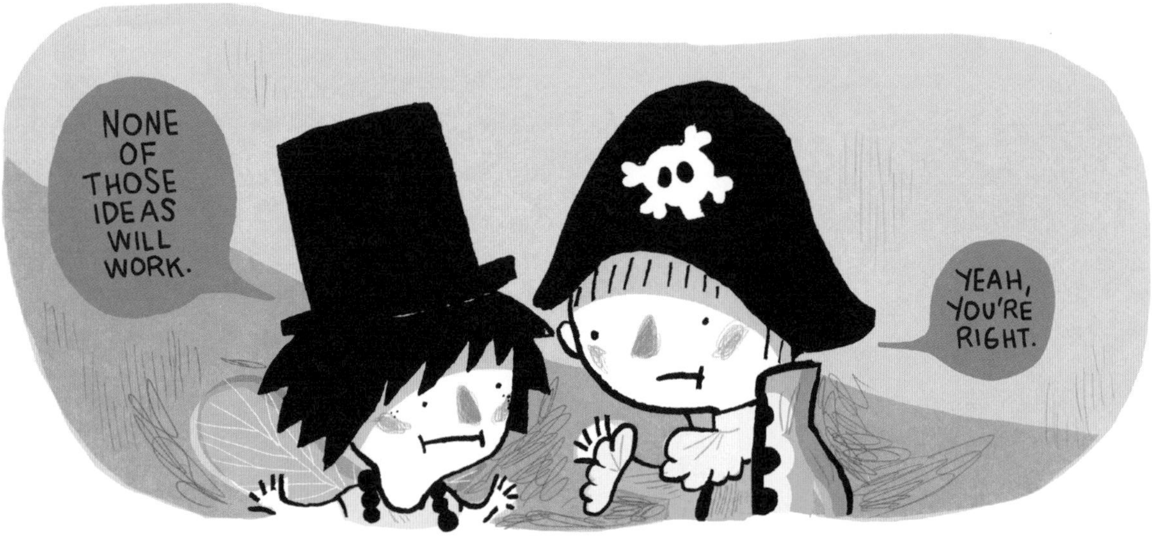
NONE OF THOSE IDEAS WILL WORK.
YEAH, YOU'RE RIGHT.

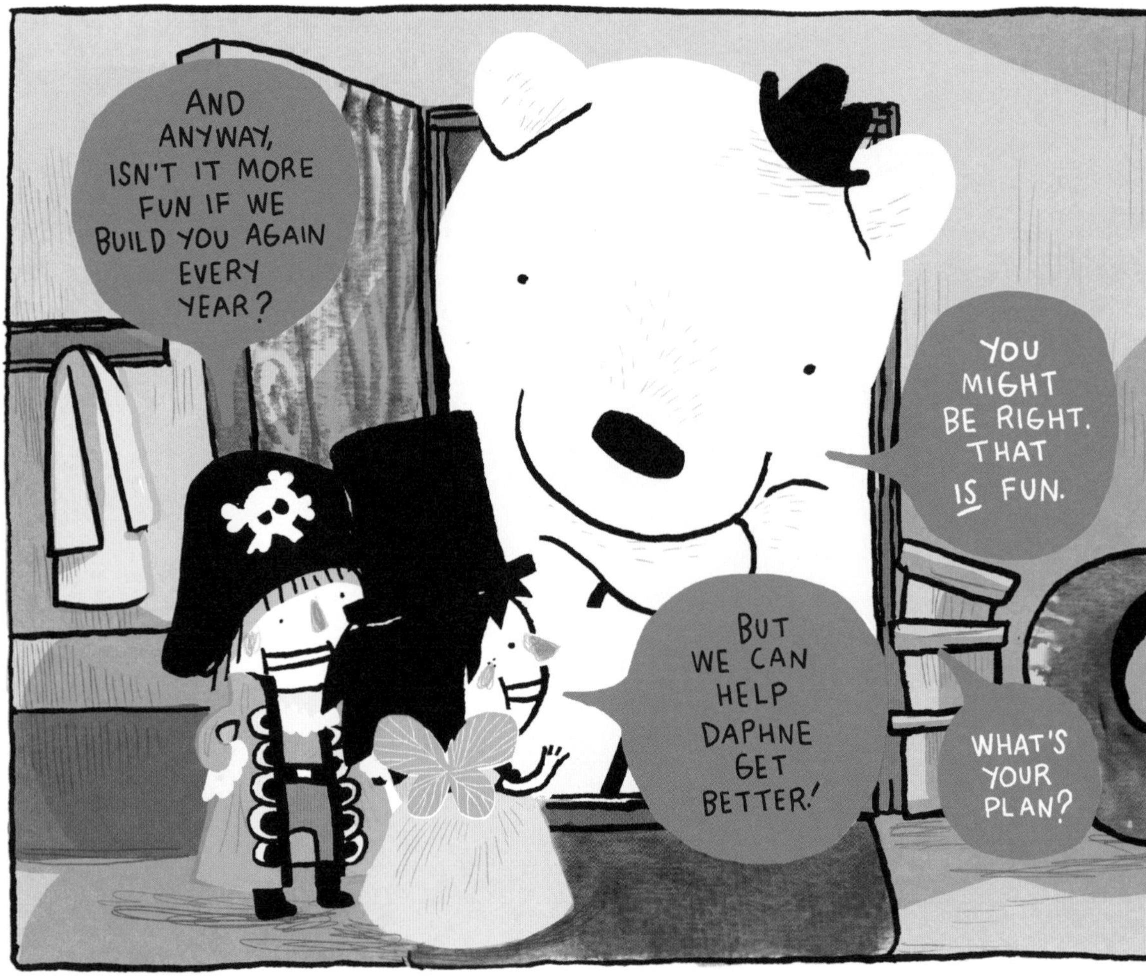
AND ANYWAY, ISN'T IT MORE FUN IF WE BUILD YOU AGAIN EVERY YEAR?
YOU MIGHT BE RIGHT. THAT IS FUN.
BUT WE CAN HELP DAPHNE GET BETTER!
WHAT'S YOUR PLAN?

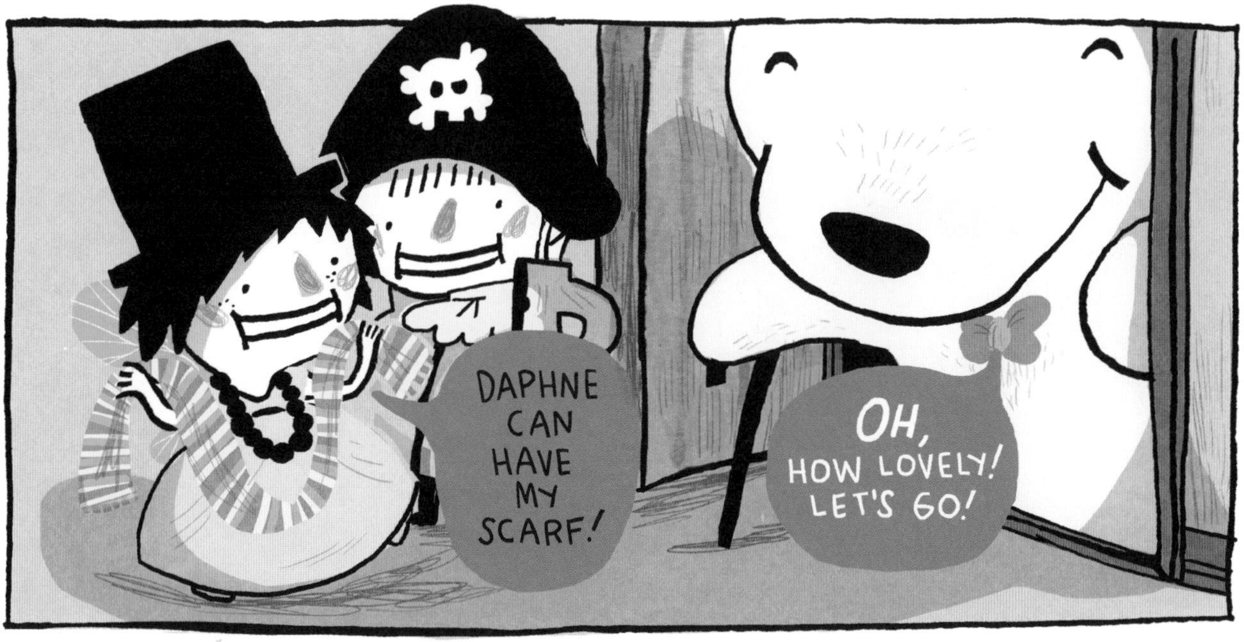
DAPHNE CAN HAVE MY SCARF!
OH, HOW LOVELY! LET'S GO!

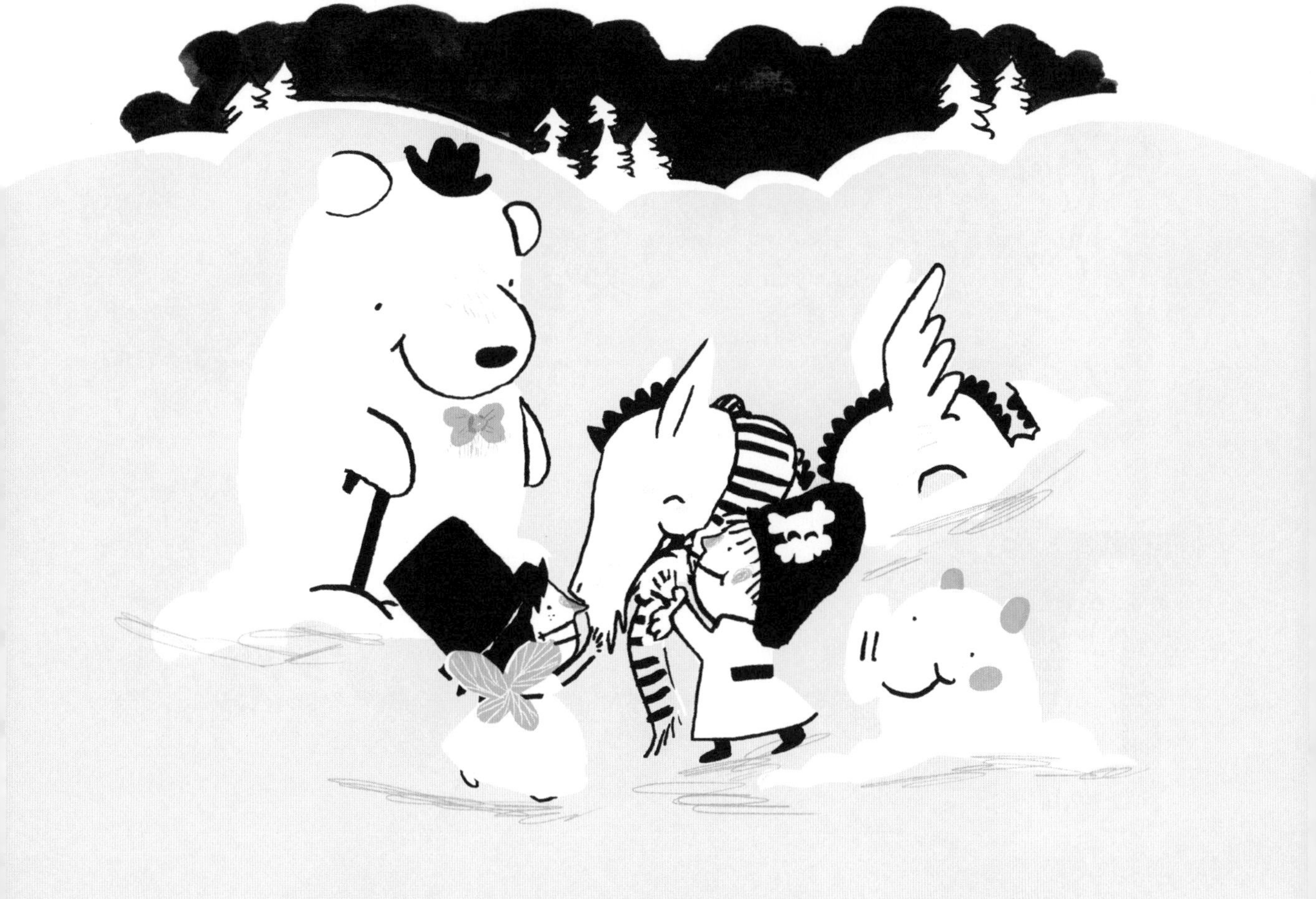

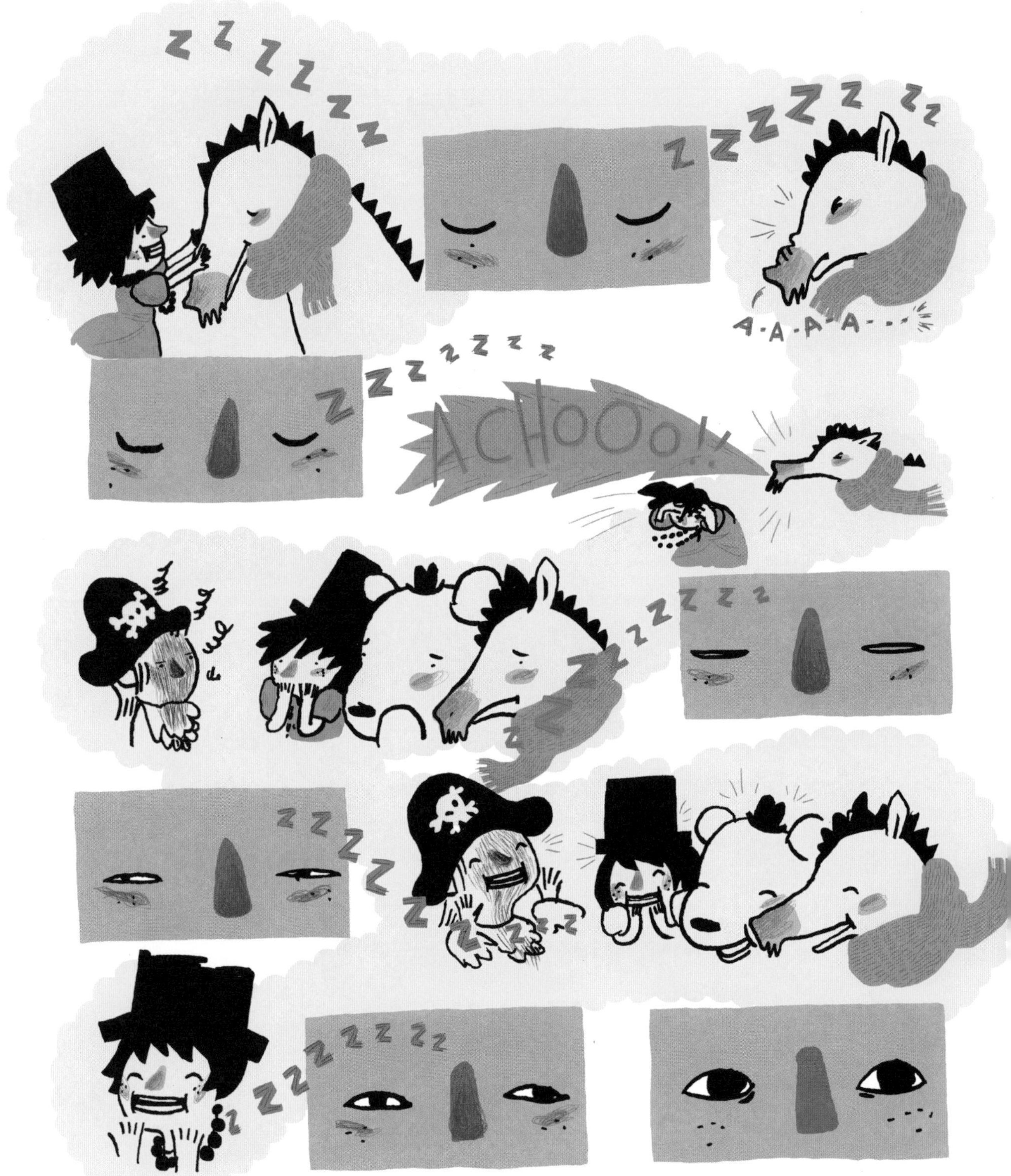

A-A-A-A
ACHOOO!!

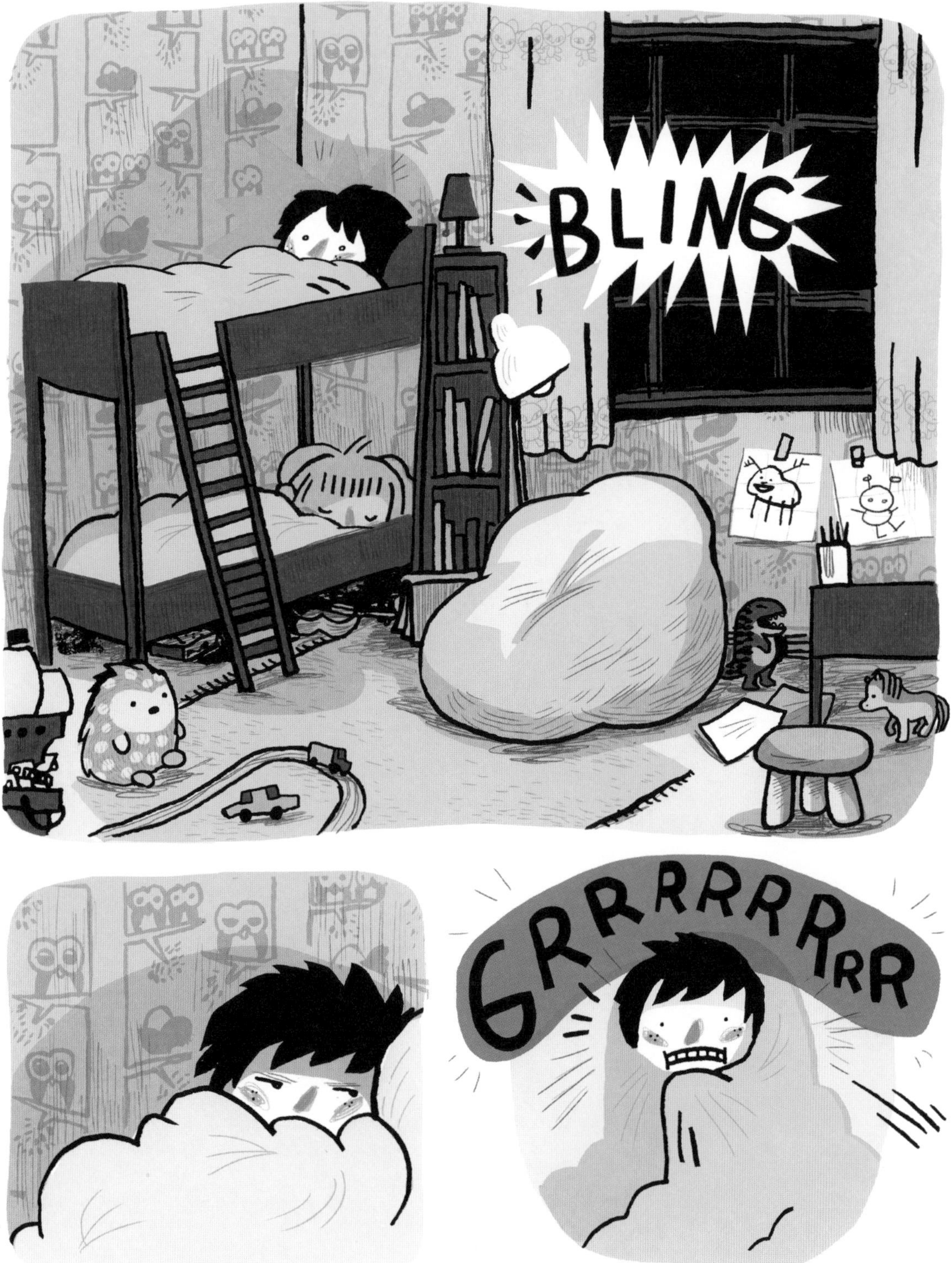
BLING
GRRRRRRRrrR

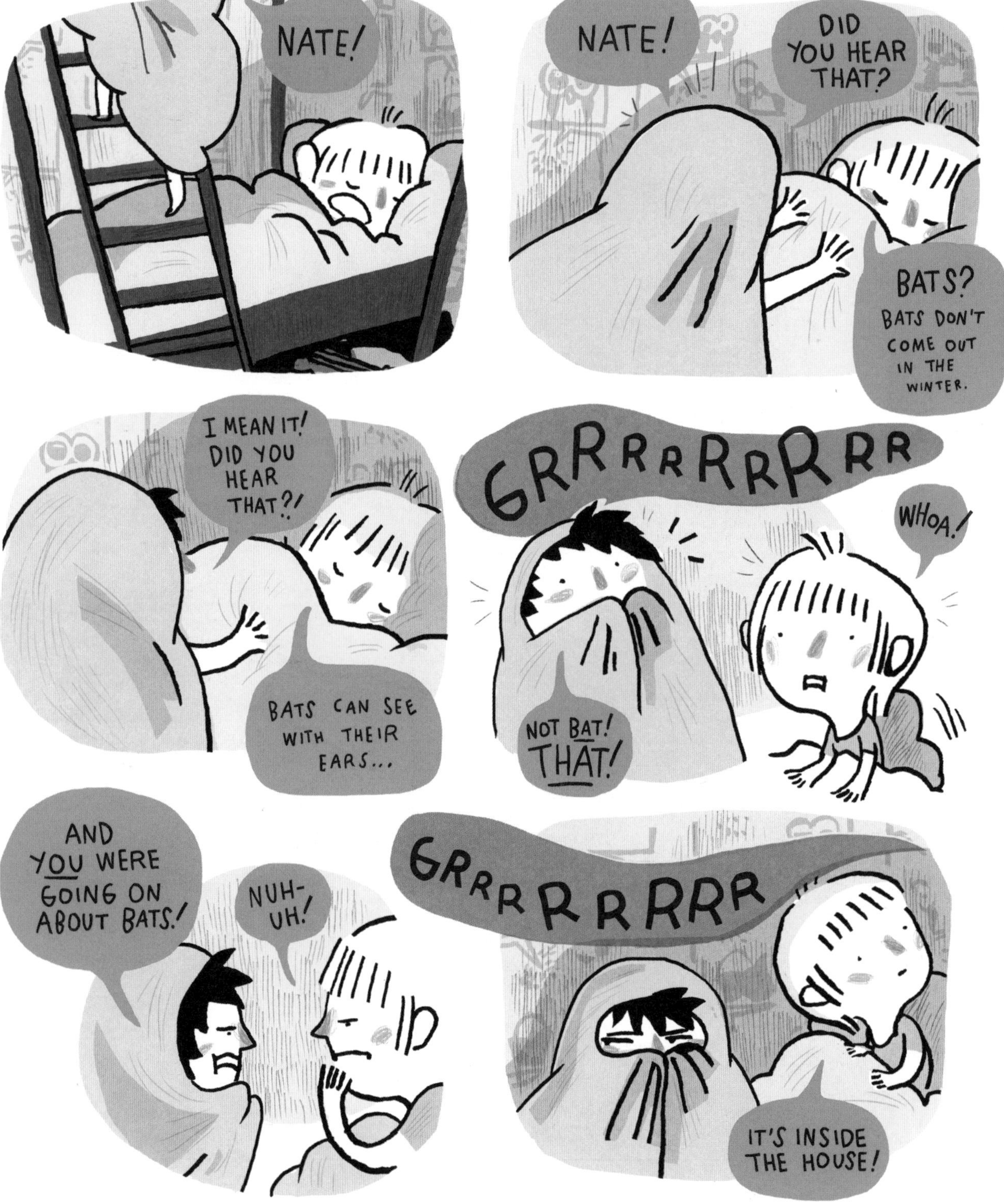
NATE!
NATE!
DID YOU HEAR THAT?
BATS? BATS DON'T COME OUT IN THE WINTER.
I MEAN IT! DID YOU HEAR THAT?!
BATS CAN SEE WITH THEIR EARS...
GRRRRRRRRRR
WHOA!
NOT BAT! THAT!
AND YOU WERE GOING ON ABOUT BATS!
NUH-UH!
GRRRRRRRRR
IT'S INSIDE THE HOUSE!

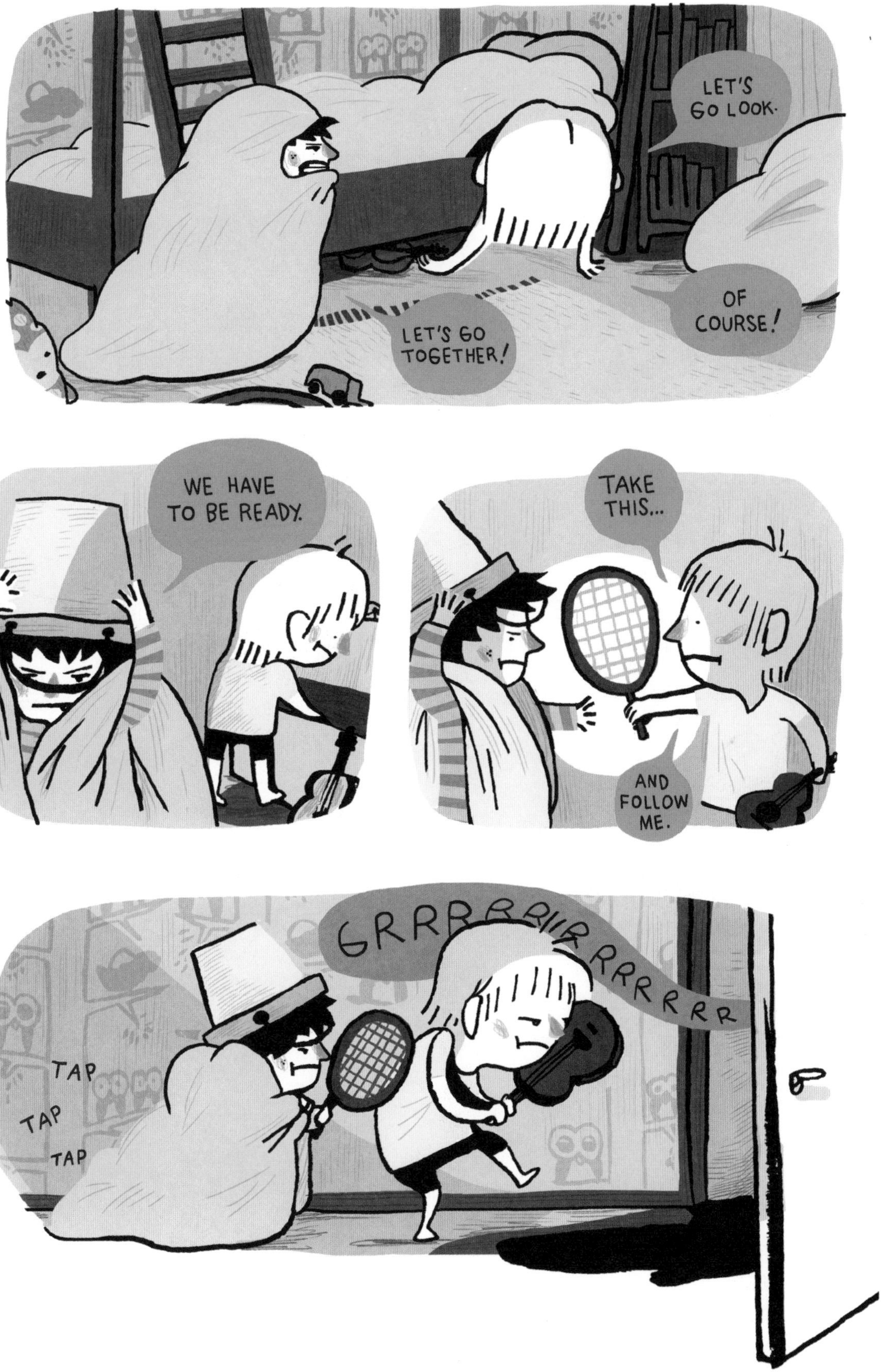
LET'S GO LOOK.
LET'S GO TOGETHER!
OF COURSE!
WE HAVE TO BE READY.
TAKE THIS...
AND FOLLOW ME.
GRRRRRRRRRRRRRR
TAP
TAP
TAP

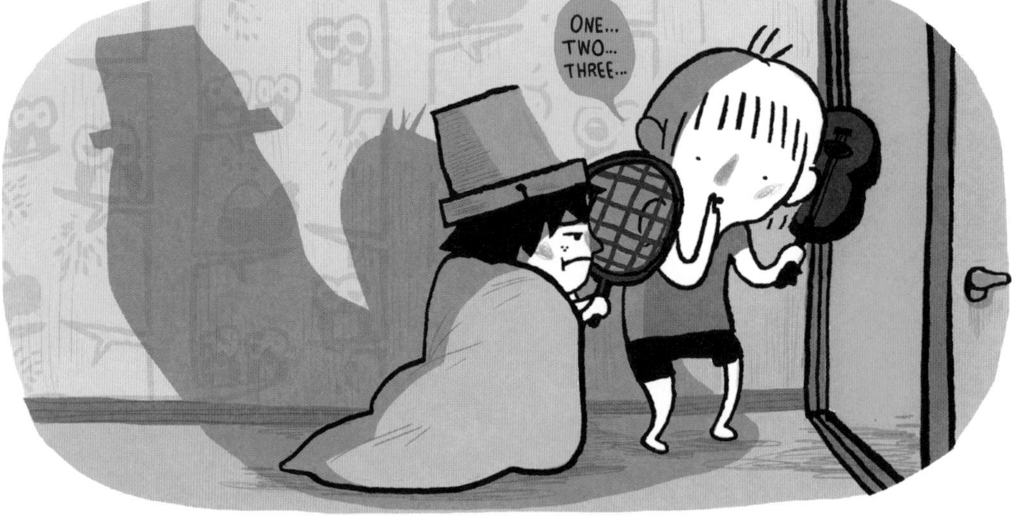
ONE... TWO... THREE...

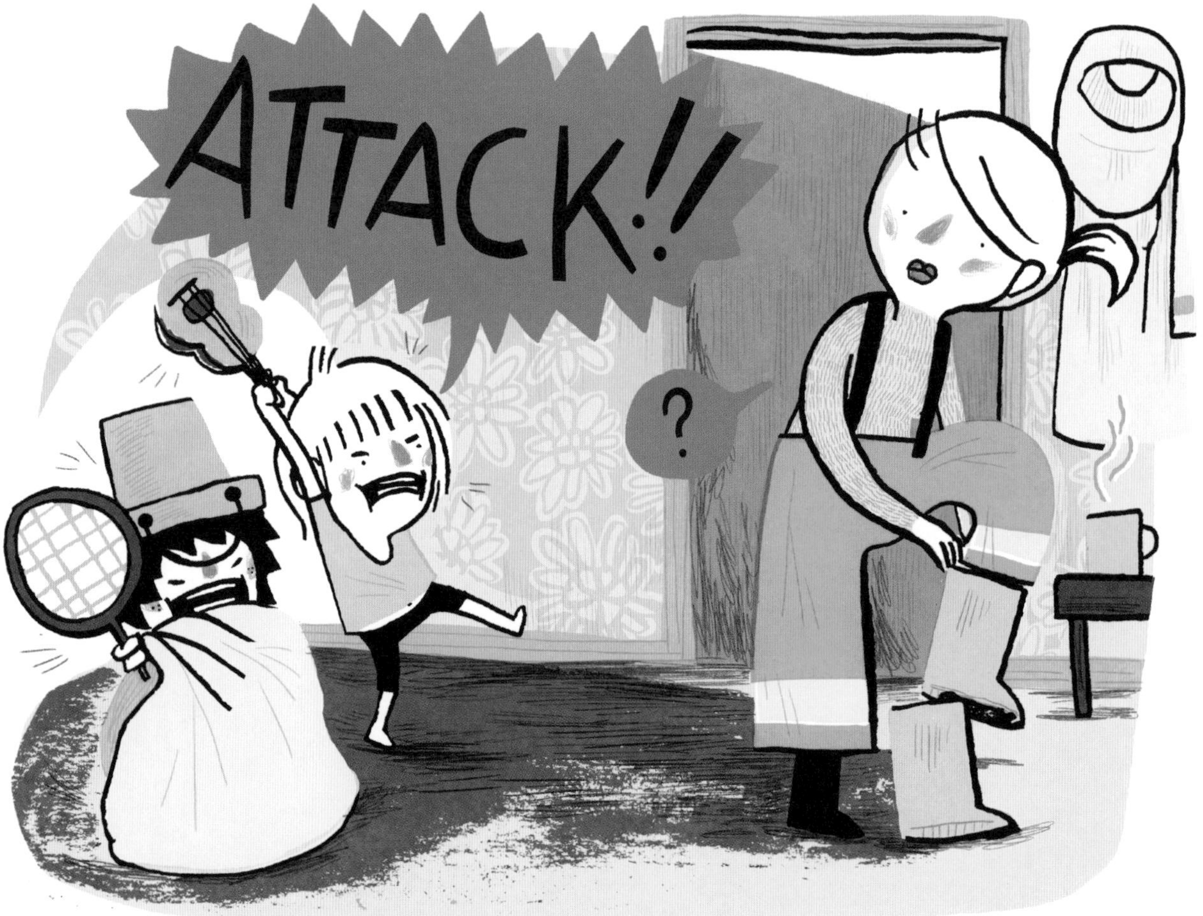
ATTACK!!
?

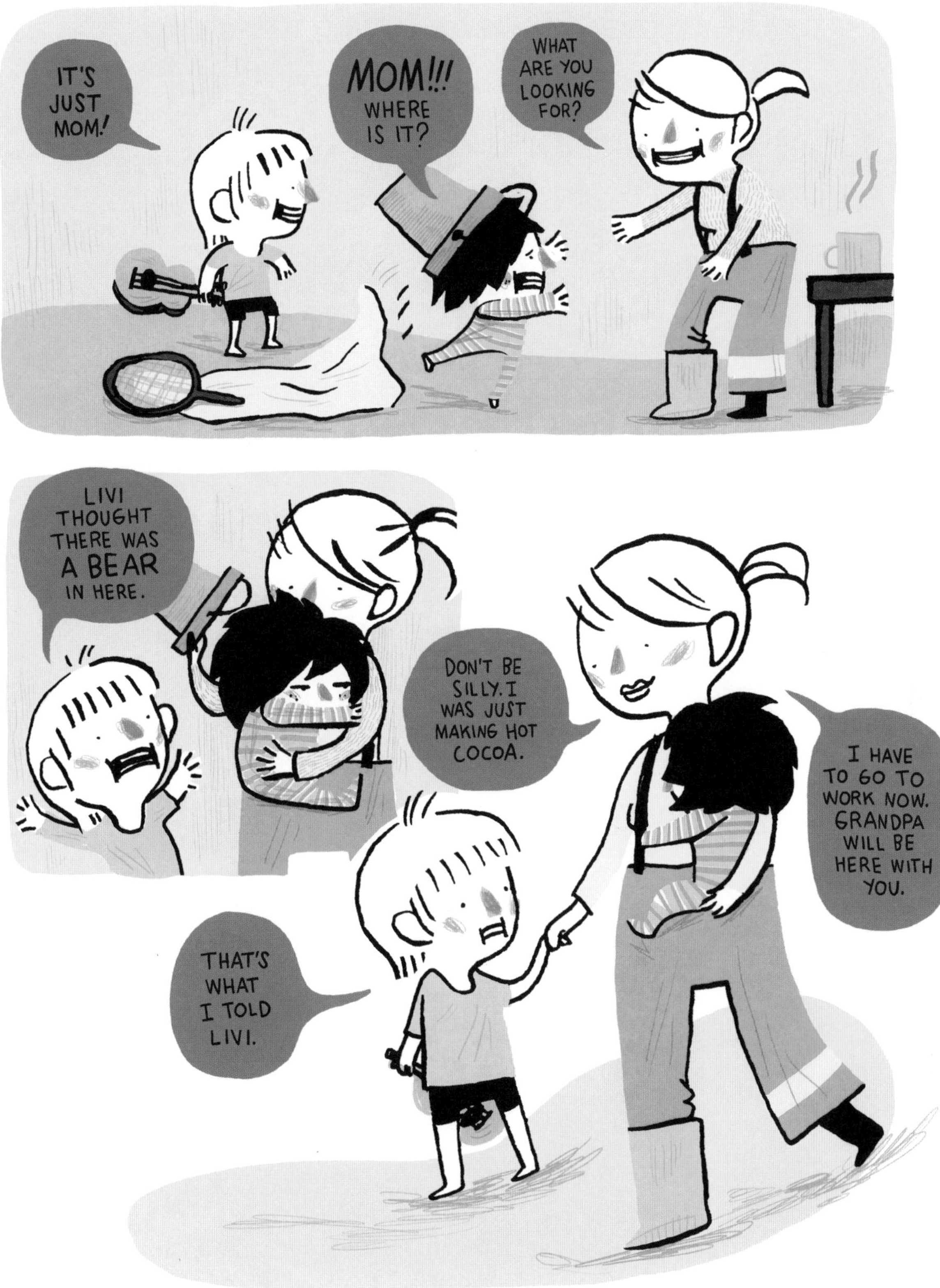
IT'S JUST MOM!
MOM!!! WHERE IS IT?
WHAT ARE YOU LOOKING FOR?
LIVI THOUGHT THERE WAS A BEAR IN HERE.
DON'T BE SILLY. I WAS JUST MAKING HOT COCOA.
I HAVE TO GO TO WORK NOW. GRANDPA WILL BE HERE WITH YOU.
THAT'S WHAT I TOLD LIVI.

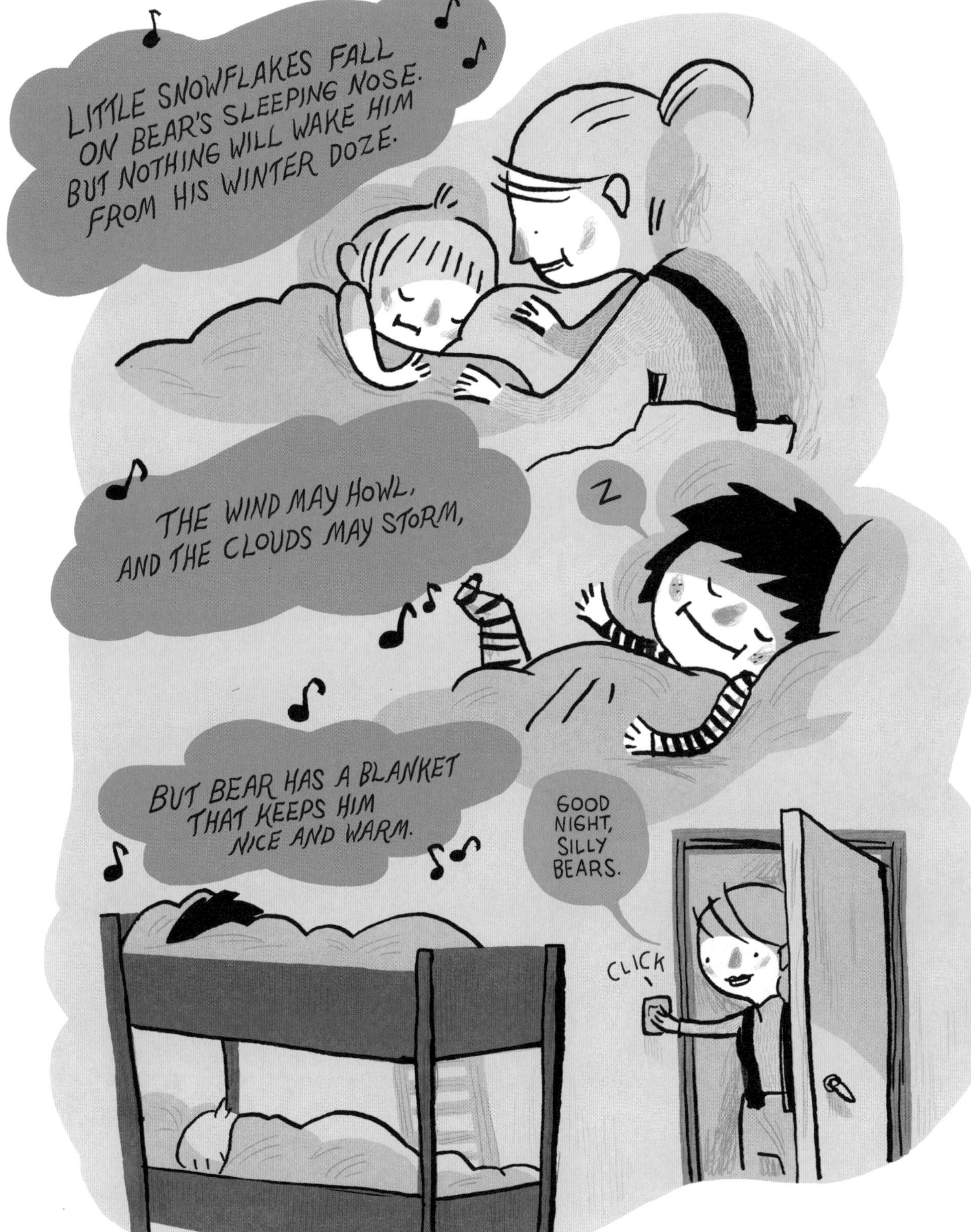
LITTLE SNOWFLAKES FALL ON BEAR'S SLEEPING NOSE. BUT NOTHING WILL WAKE HIM FROM HIS WINTER DOZE.
THE WIND MAY HOWL, AND THE CLOUDS MAY STORM,
Z
BUT BEAR HAS A BLANKET THAT KEEPS HIM NICE AND WARM.
GOOD NIGHT, SILLY BEARS.
CLICK

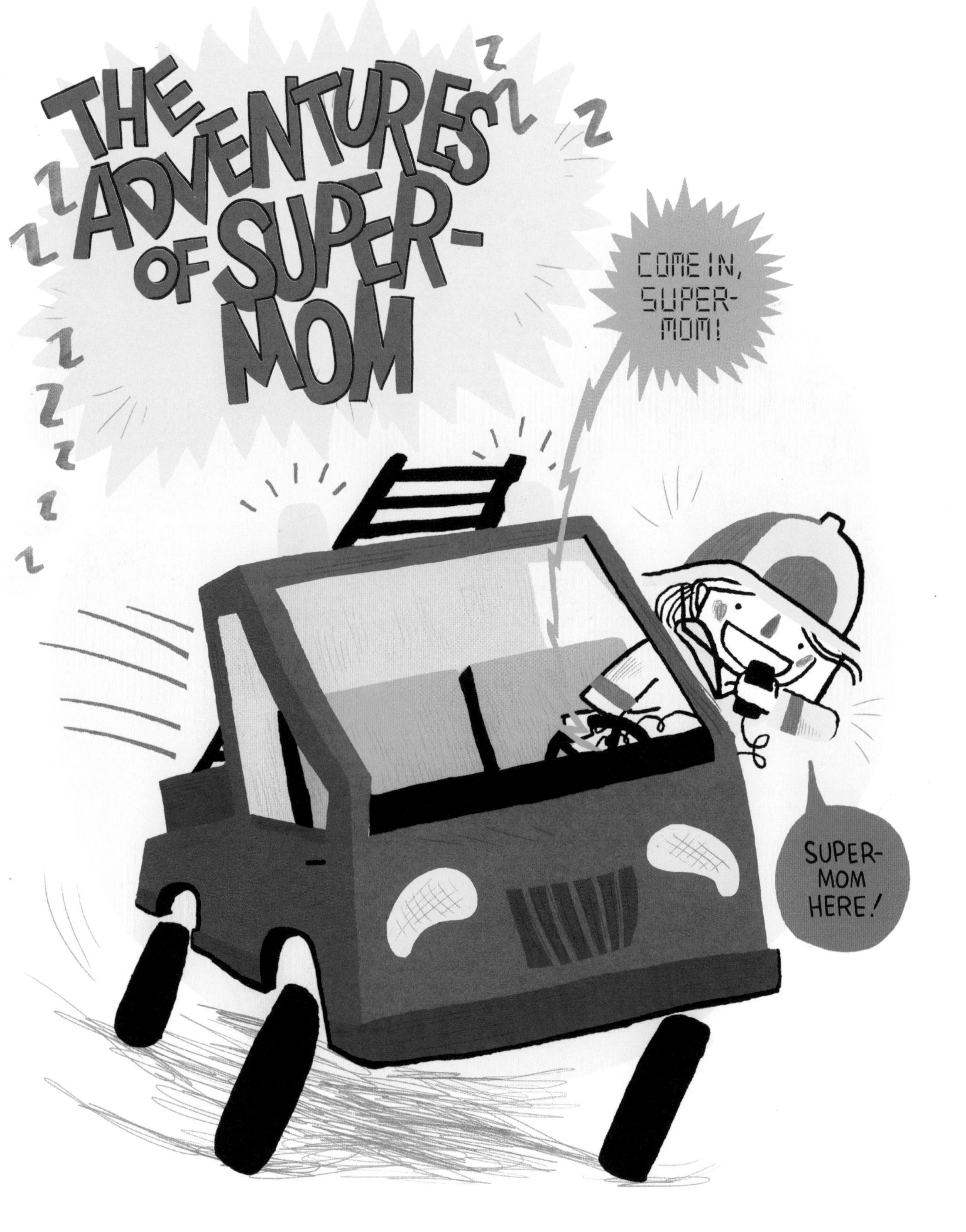
THE ADVENTURES OF SUPER-MOM
COME IN, SUPER-MOM!
SUPER-MOM HERE!

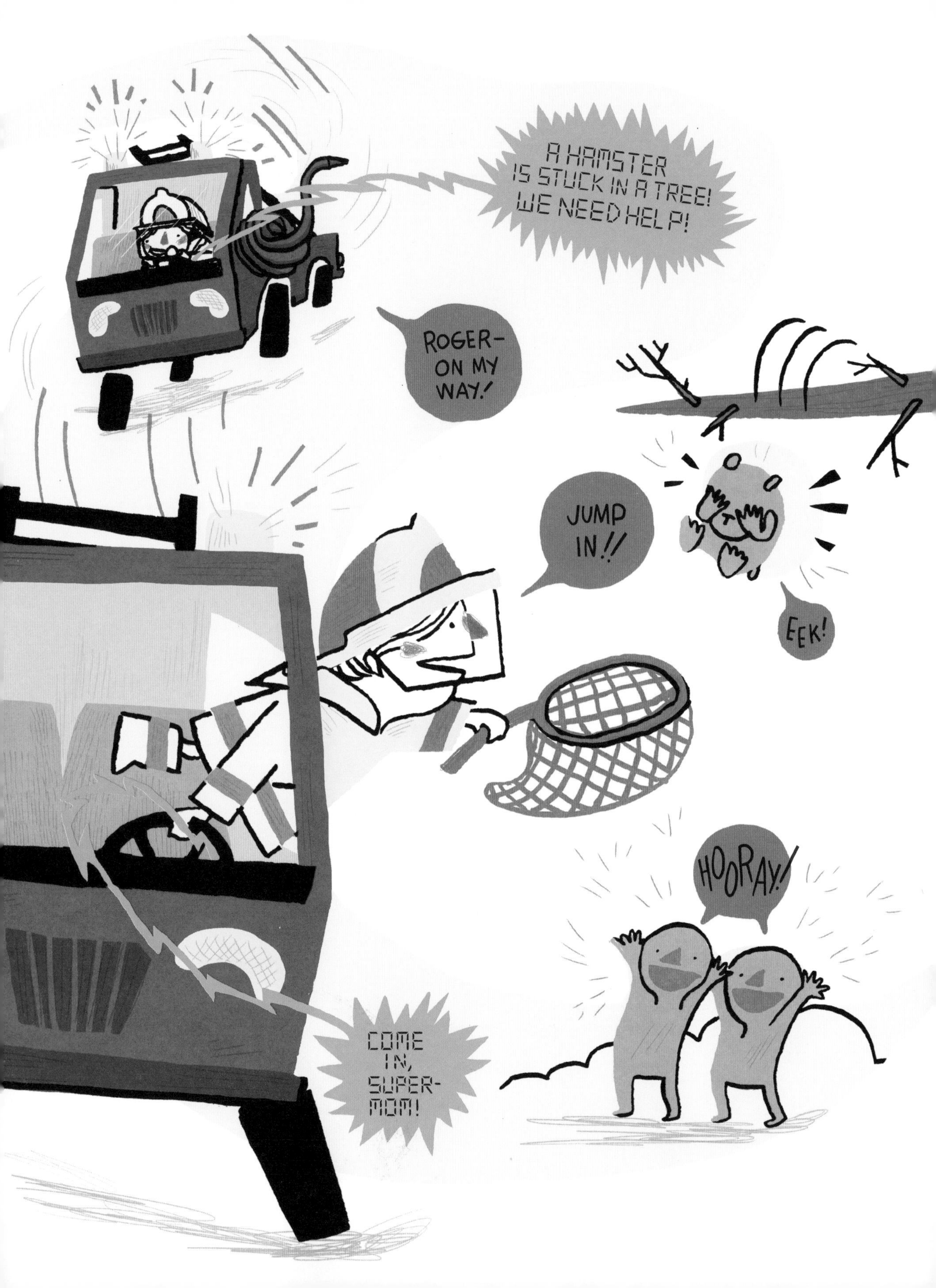
A HAMSTER IS STUCK IN A TREE! WE NEED HELP!
ROGER—ON MY WAY!
JUMP IN!!
EEK!
HOORAY!
COME IN, SUPER-MOM!

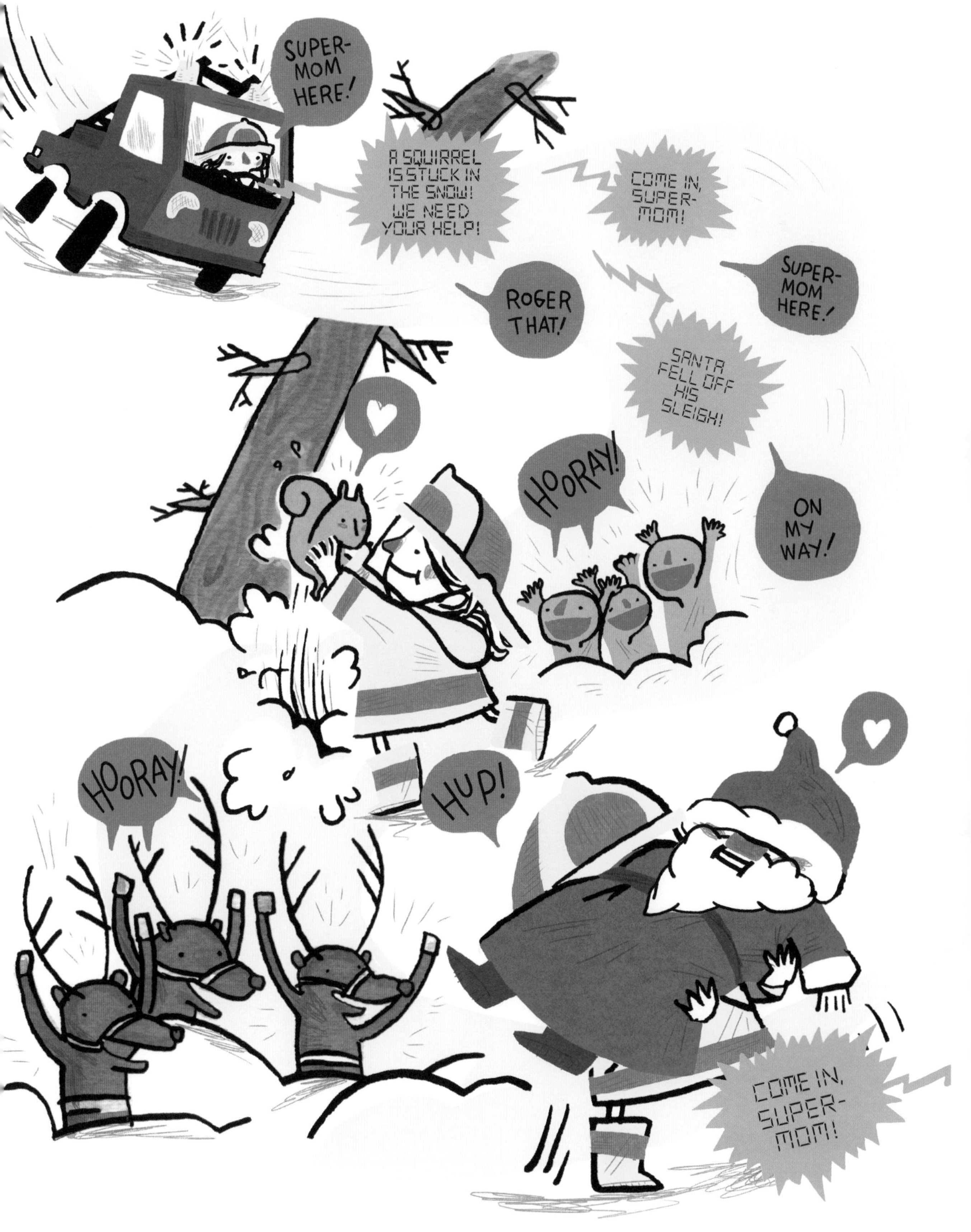

SUPER-MOM HERE!
A SQUIRREL IS STUCK IN THE SNOW! WE NEED YOUR HELP!
ROGER THAT!
COME IN, SUPER-MOM!
SUPER-MOM HERE!
SANTA FELL OFF HIS SLEIGH!
HOORAY!
ON MY WAY!
HOORAY!
HUP!
COME IN, SUPER-MOM!

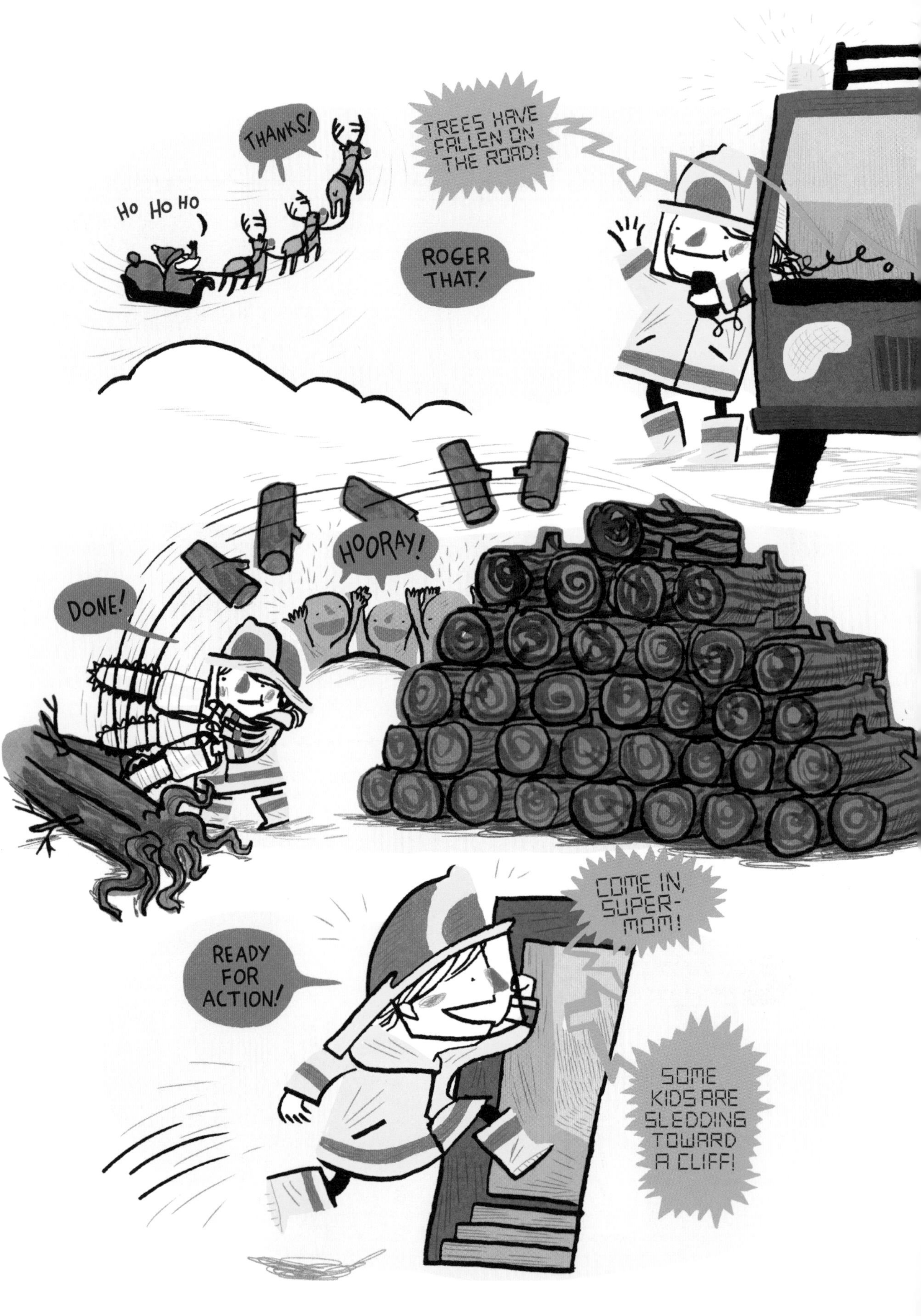
TREES HAVE FALLEN ON THE ROAD!
THANKS!
HO HO HO
ROGER THAT!
HOORAY!
DONE!
COME IN, SUPER-MOM!
READY FOR ACTION!
SOME KIDS ARE SLEDDING TOWARD A CLIFF!

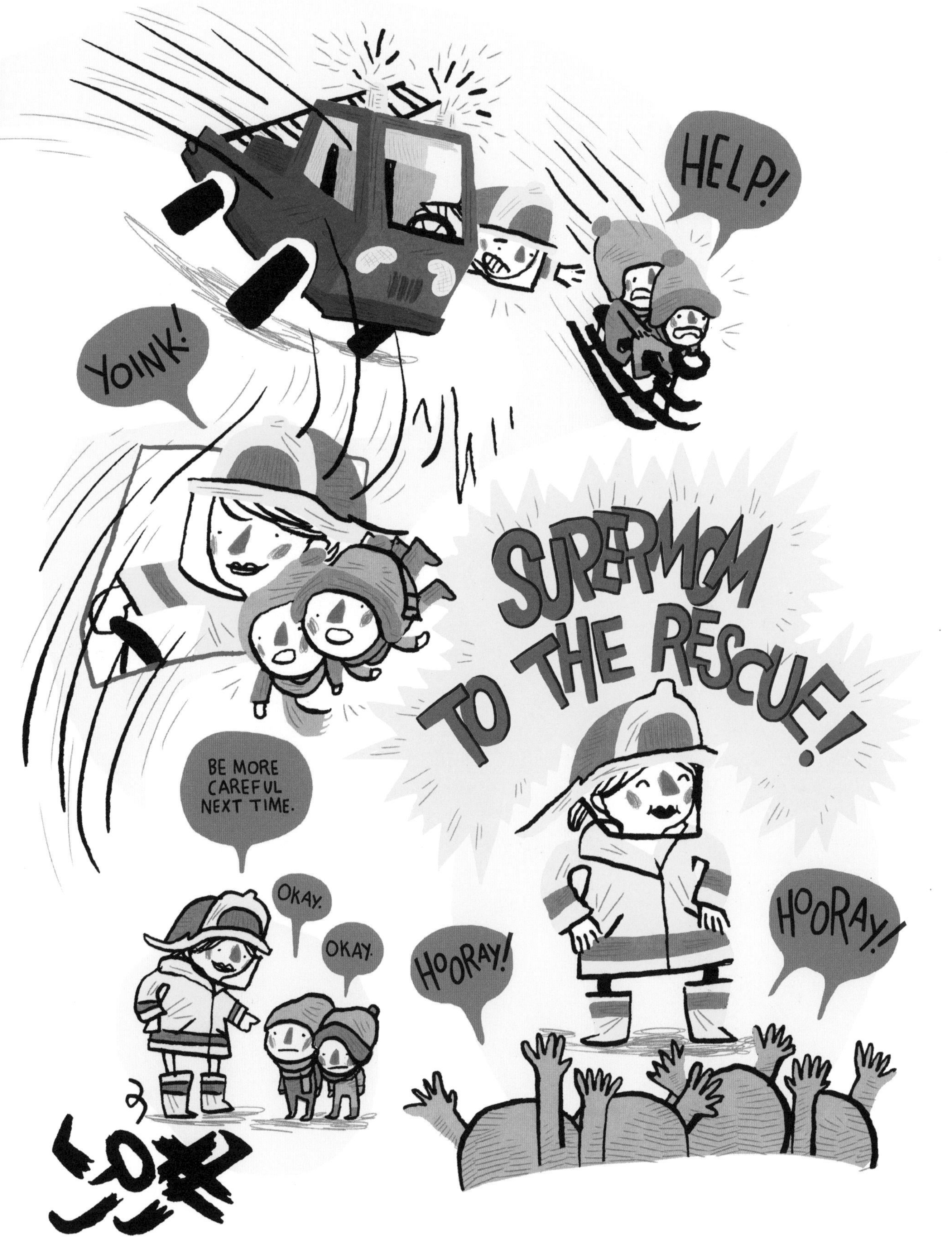
HELP!
YOINK!
SUPERMOM TO THE RESCUE!
BE MORE CAREFUL NEXT TIME.
OKAY.
OKAY.
HOORAY!
HOORAY!

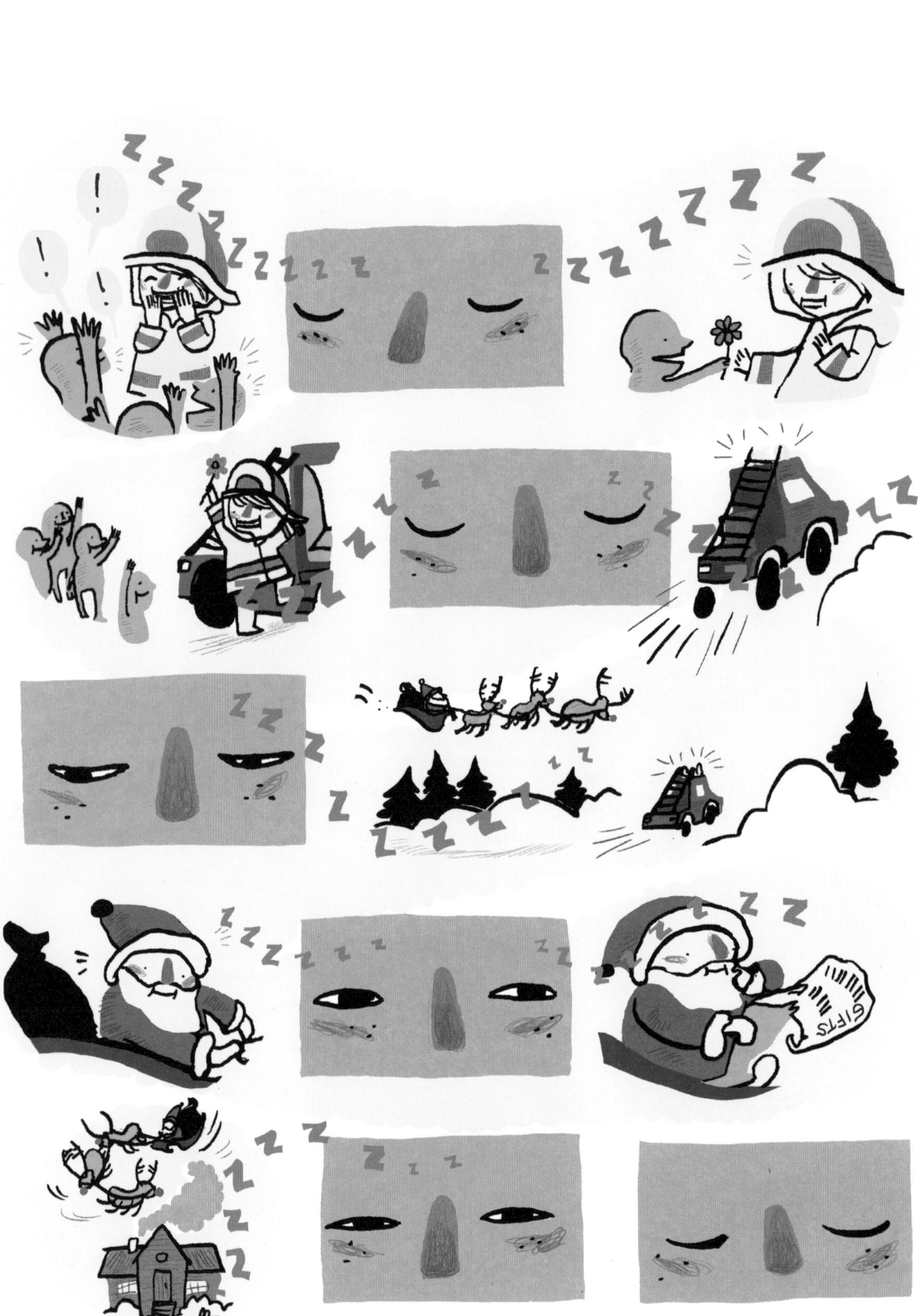
GIFTS

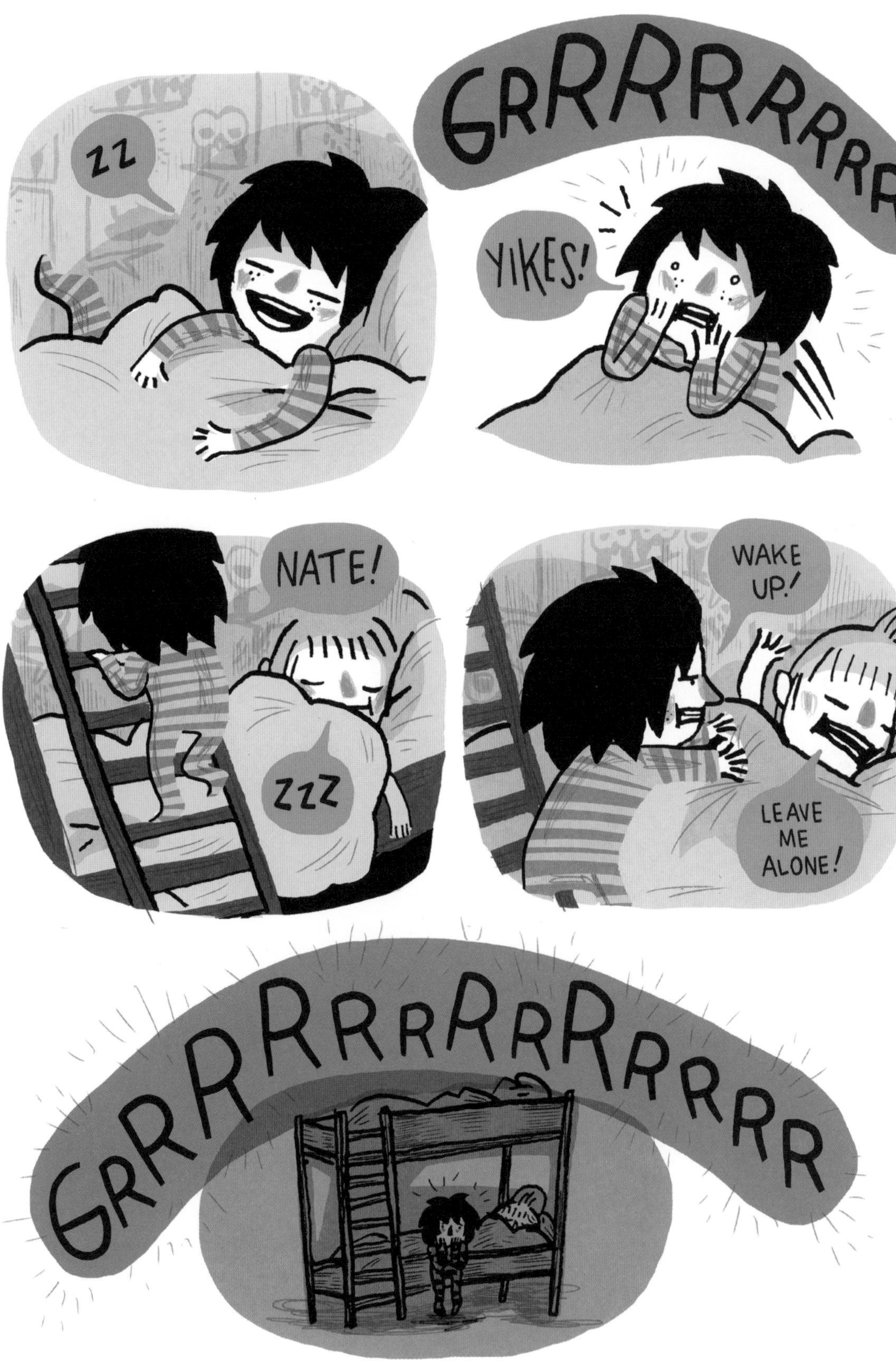
ZZ
GRRRRRRRR
YIKES!
NATE!
ZZZ
WAKE UP!
LEAVE ME ALONE!
GRRRRRRRRRRRRRRR

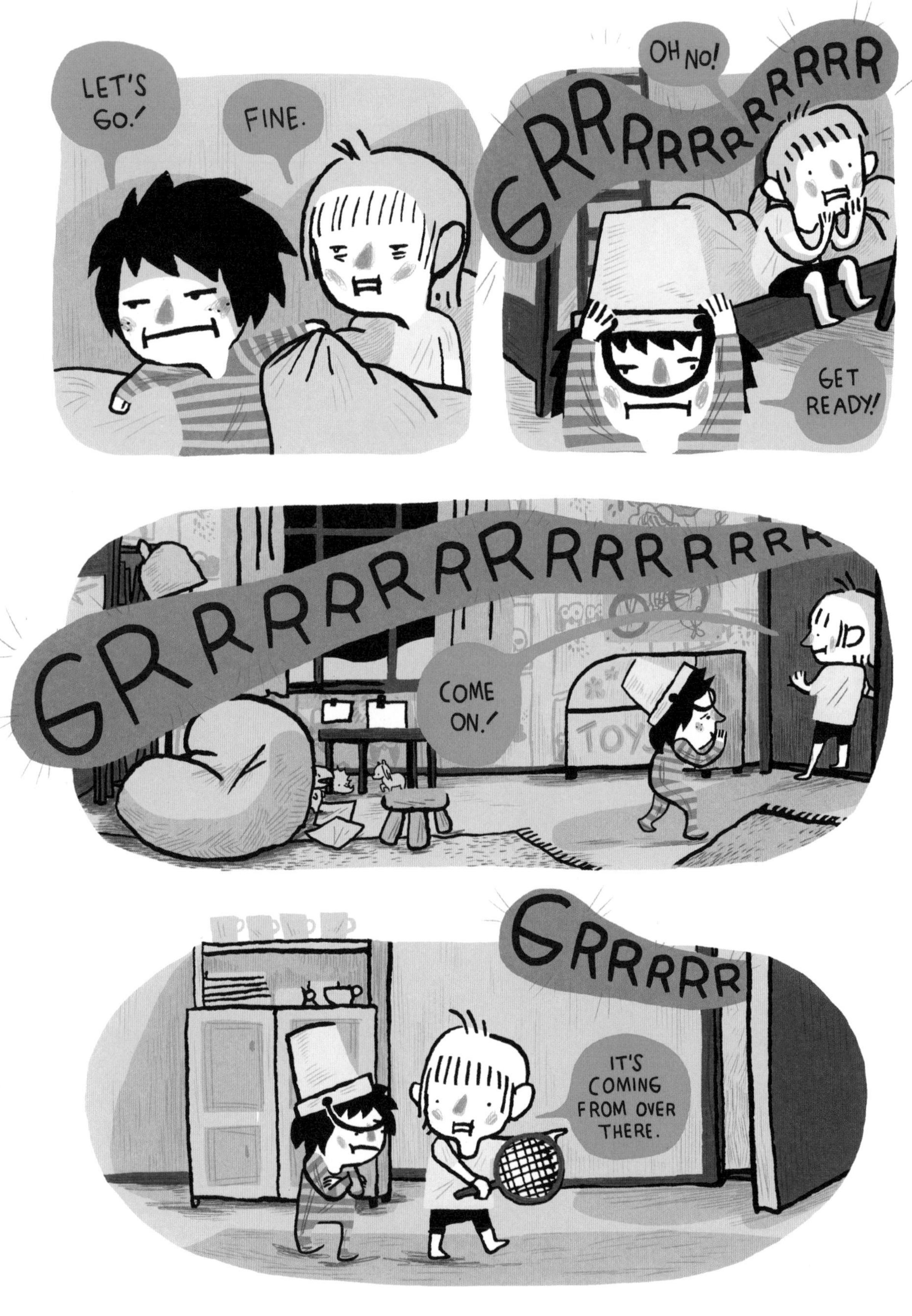
LET'S GO!
FINE.
OH NO!
GRRRRRRRRRRRR
GET READY!
GRRRRRRRRRRRRRRR
COME ON!
TOYS
GRRRRRR
IT'S COMING FROM OVER THERE.

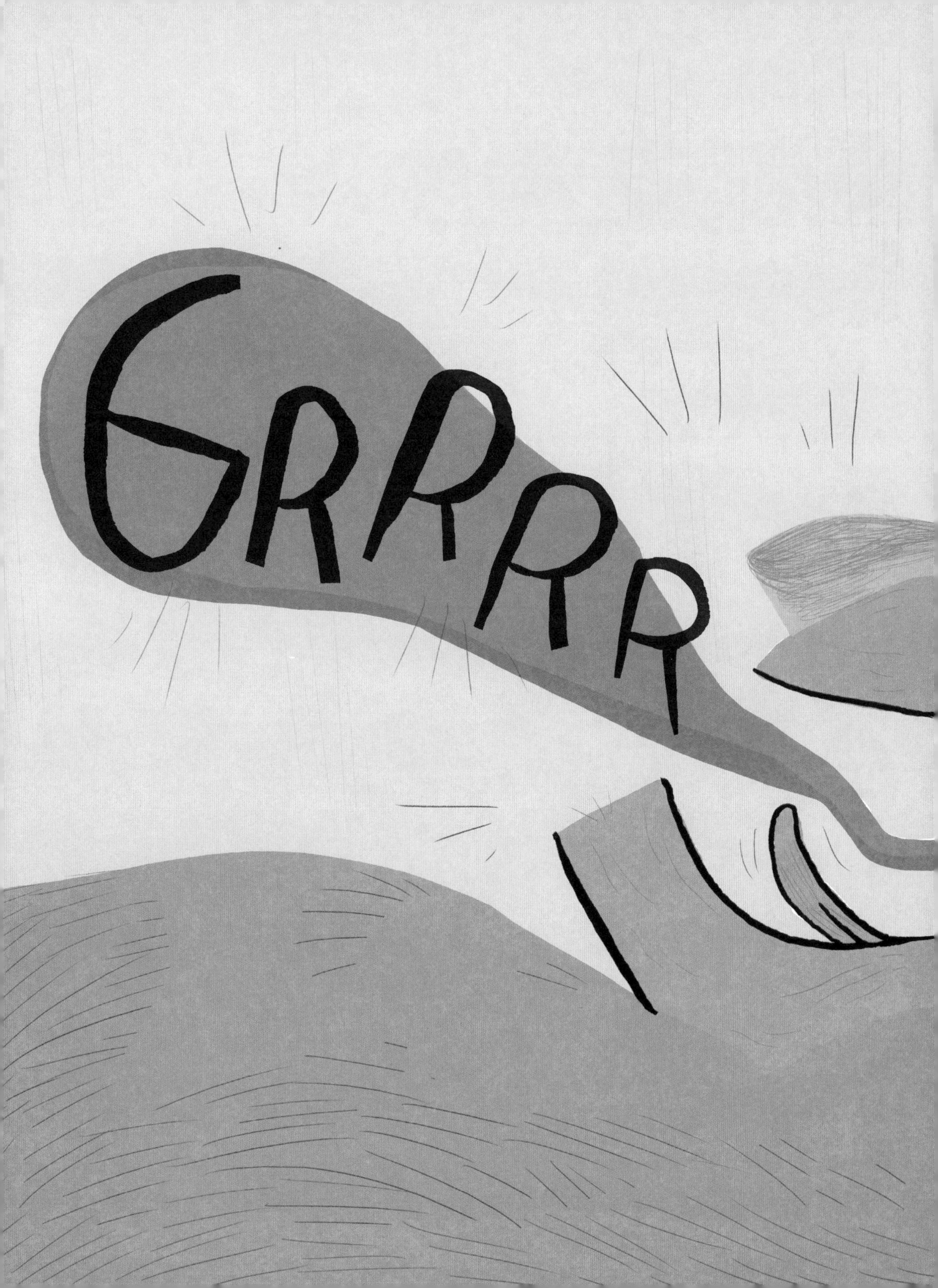
GRRRR

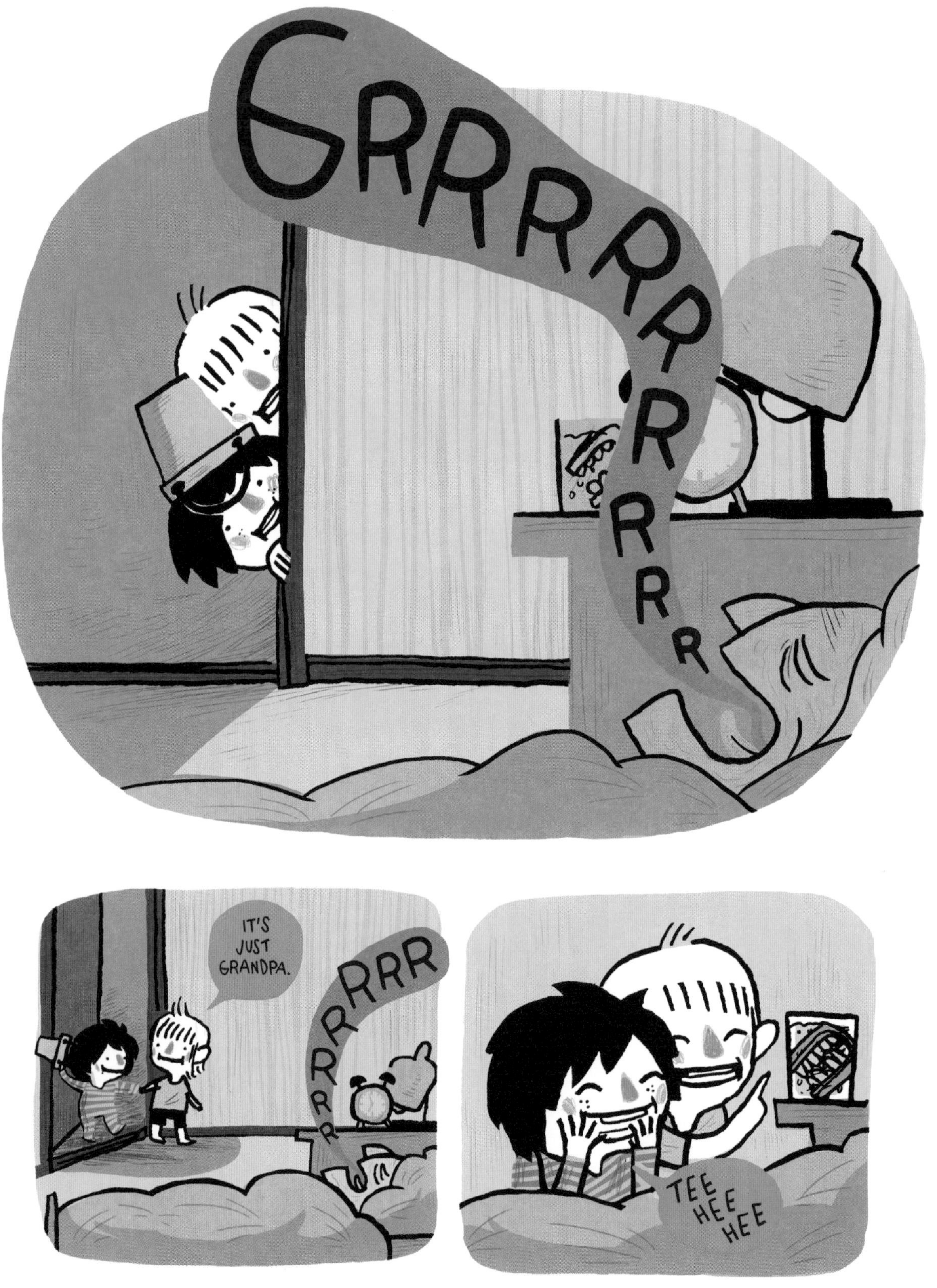
GRRRRRRRRRRR
IT'S JUST GRANDPA.
RRRRRR
TEE HEE HEE

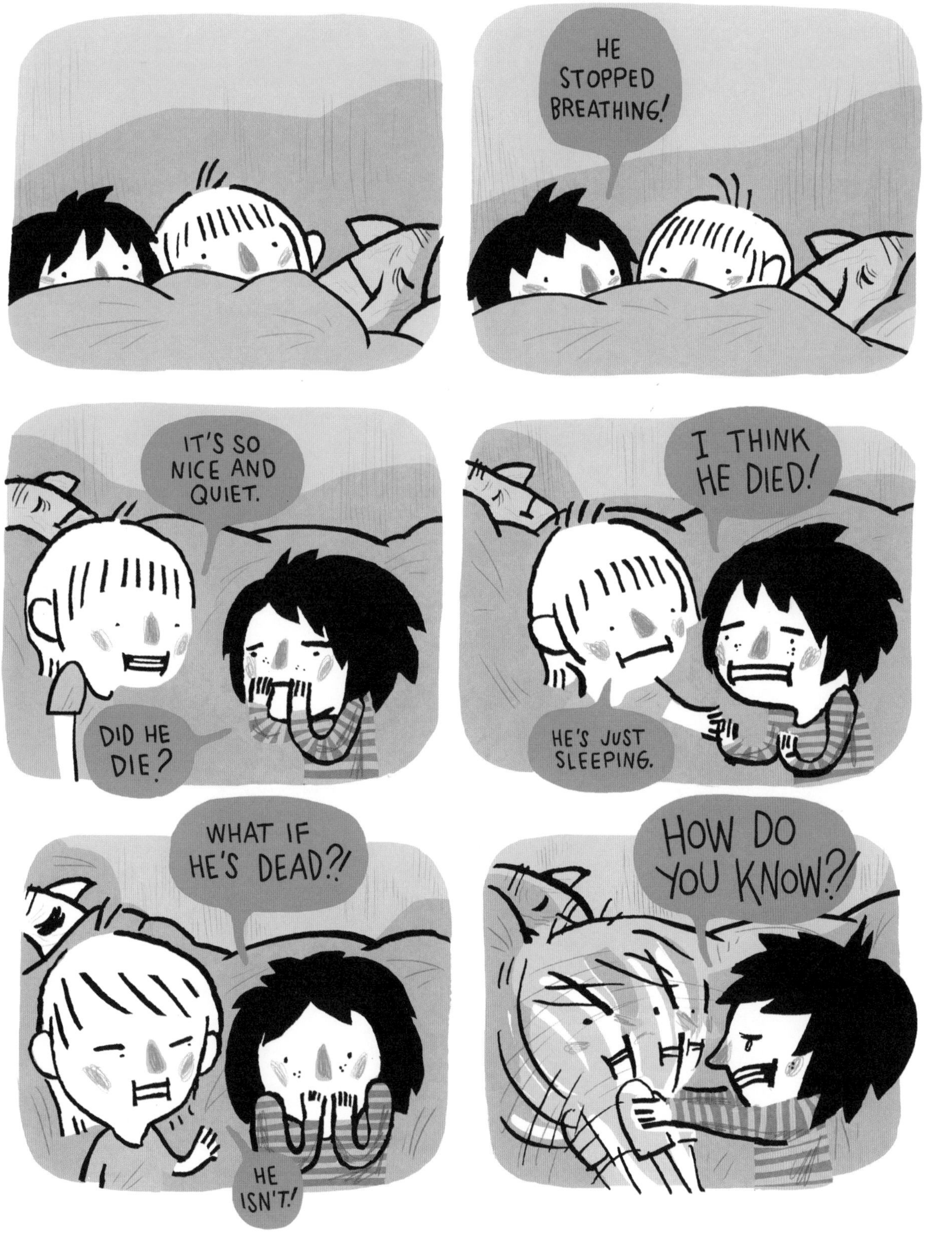
HE STOPPED BREATHING!
IT'S SO NICE AND QUIET.
DID HE DIE?
I THINK HE DIED!
HE'S JUST SLEEPING.
WHAT IF HE'S DEAD?!
HE ISN'T!
HOW DO YOU KNOW?!

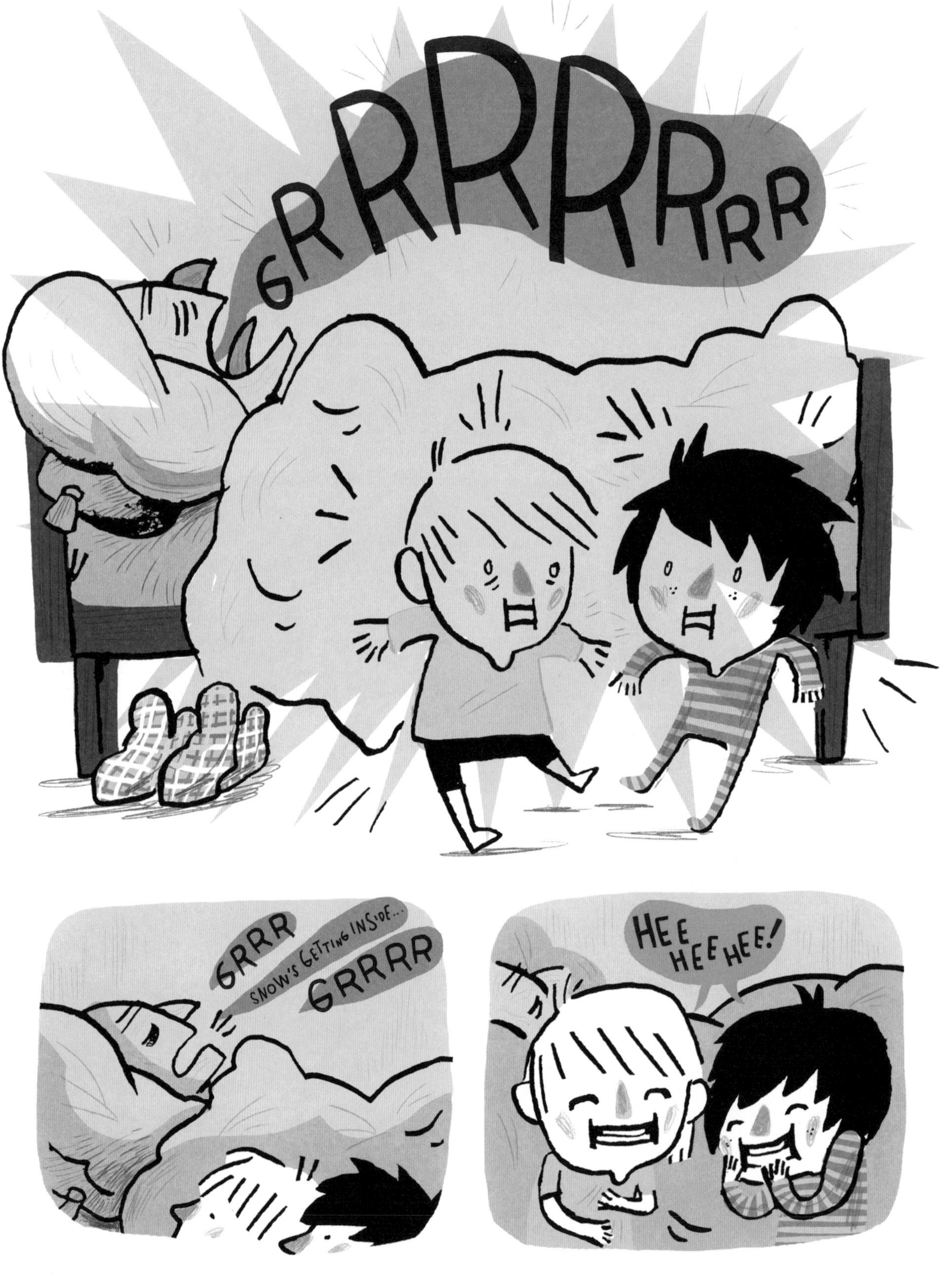
GRRRRRRRR
GRRR
SNOW'S GETTING INSIDE...
GRRRR
HEE HEE HEE!

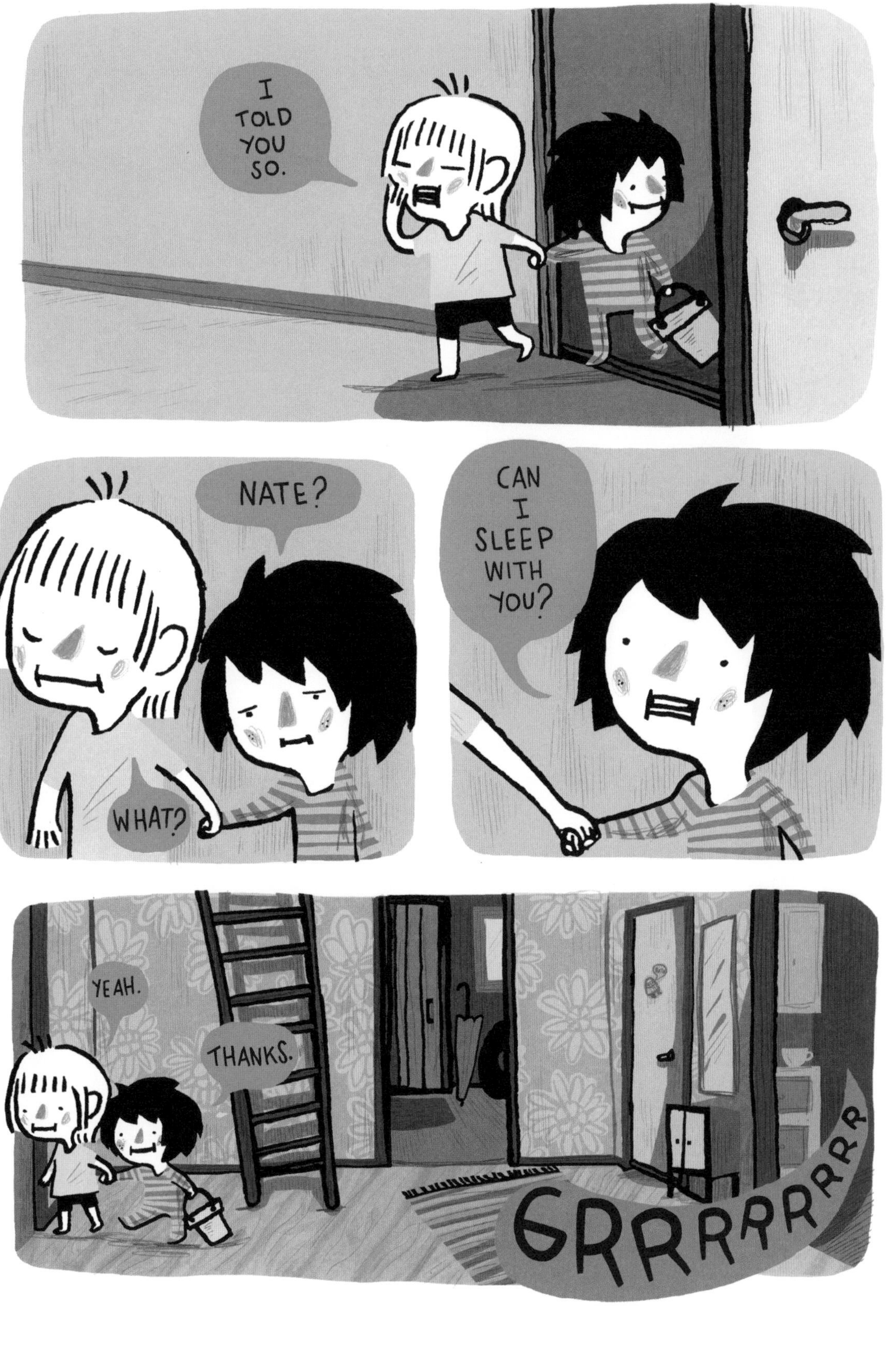
I TOLD YOU SO.
NATE?
WHAT?
CAN I SLEEP WITH YOU?
YEAH.
THANKS.
GRRRRRRRRR

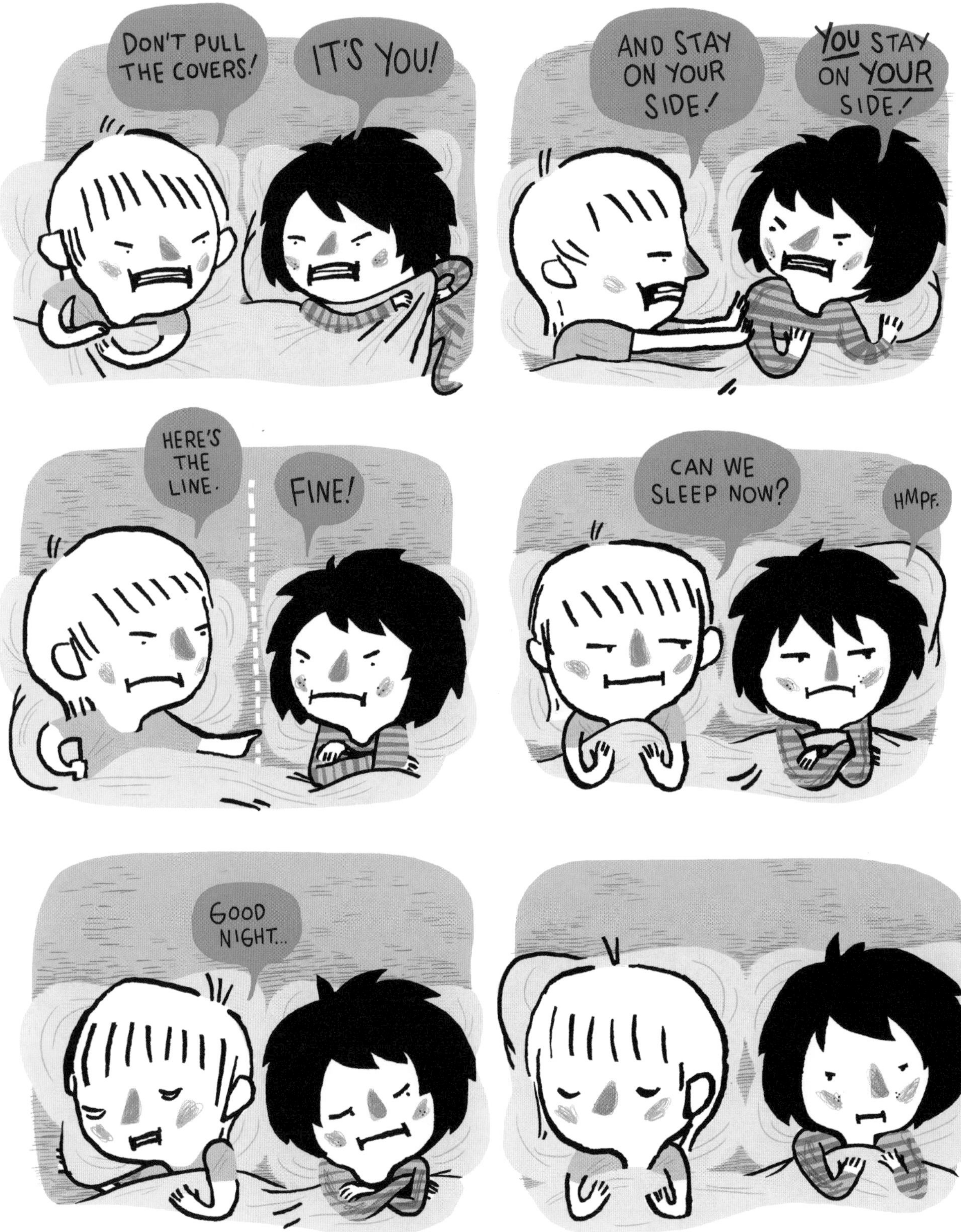
DON'T PULL THE COVERS!
IT'S YOU!
AND STAY ON YOUR SIDE!
YOU STAY ON YOUR SIDE!
HERE'S THE LINE.
FINE!
CAN WE SLEEP NOW?
HMPF.
GOOD NIGHT...

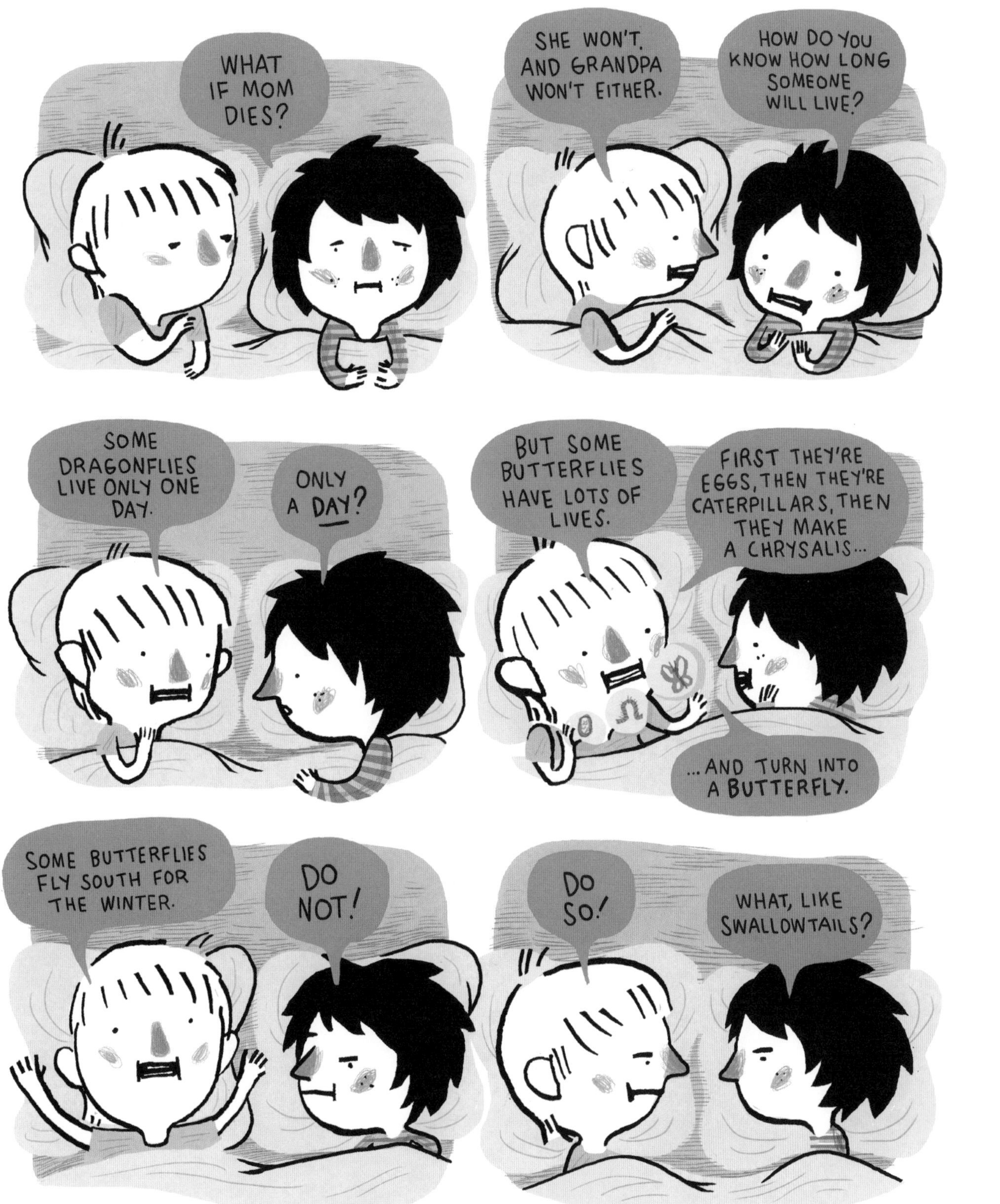
WHAT IF MOM DIES?
SHE WON'T. AND GRANDPA WON'T EITHER.
HOW DO YOU KNOW HOW LONG SOMEONE WILL LIVE?
SOME DRAGONFLIES LIVE ONLY ONE DAY.
ONLY A DAY?
BUT SOME BUTTERFLIES HAVE LOTS OF LIVES.
FIRST THEY'RE EGGS, THEN THEY'RE CATERPILLARS, THEN THEY MAKE A CHRYSALIS...
...AND TURN INTO A BUTTERFLY.
SOME BUTTERFLIES FLY SOUTH FOR THE WINTER.
DO NOT!
DO SO!
WHAT, LIKE SWALLOWTAILS?

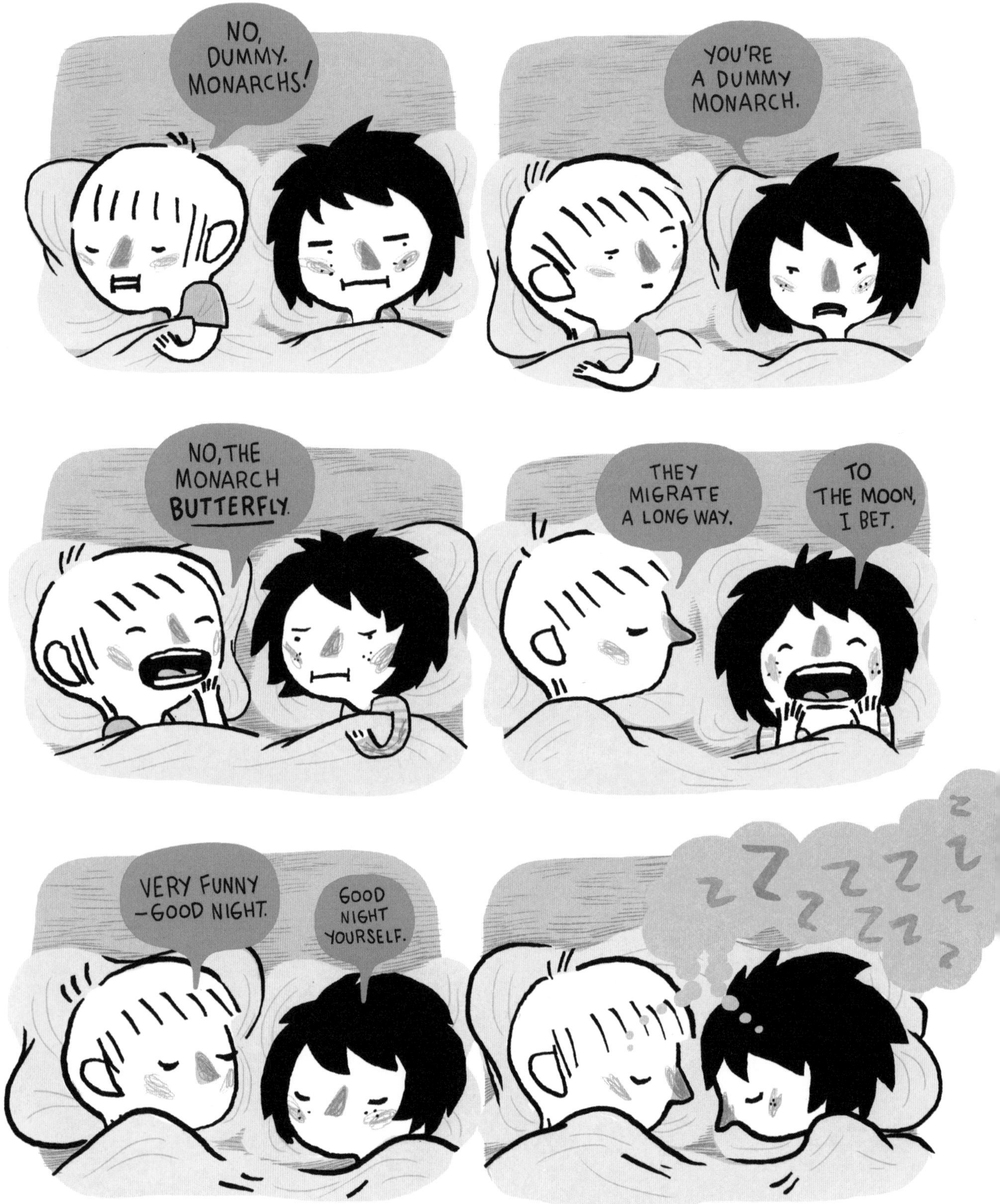
NO, DUMMY. MONARCHS!
YOU'RE A DUMMY MONARCH.
NO, THE MONARCH BUTTERFLY.
THEY MIGRATE A LONG WAY.
TO THE MOON, I BET.
VERY FUNNY —GOOD NIGHT.
GOOD NIGHT YOURSELF.
Z Z Z Z Z Z Z Z Z Z Z Z

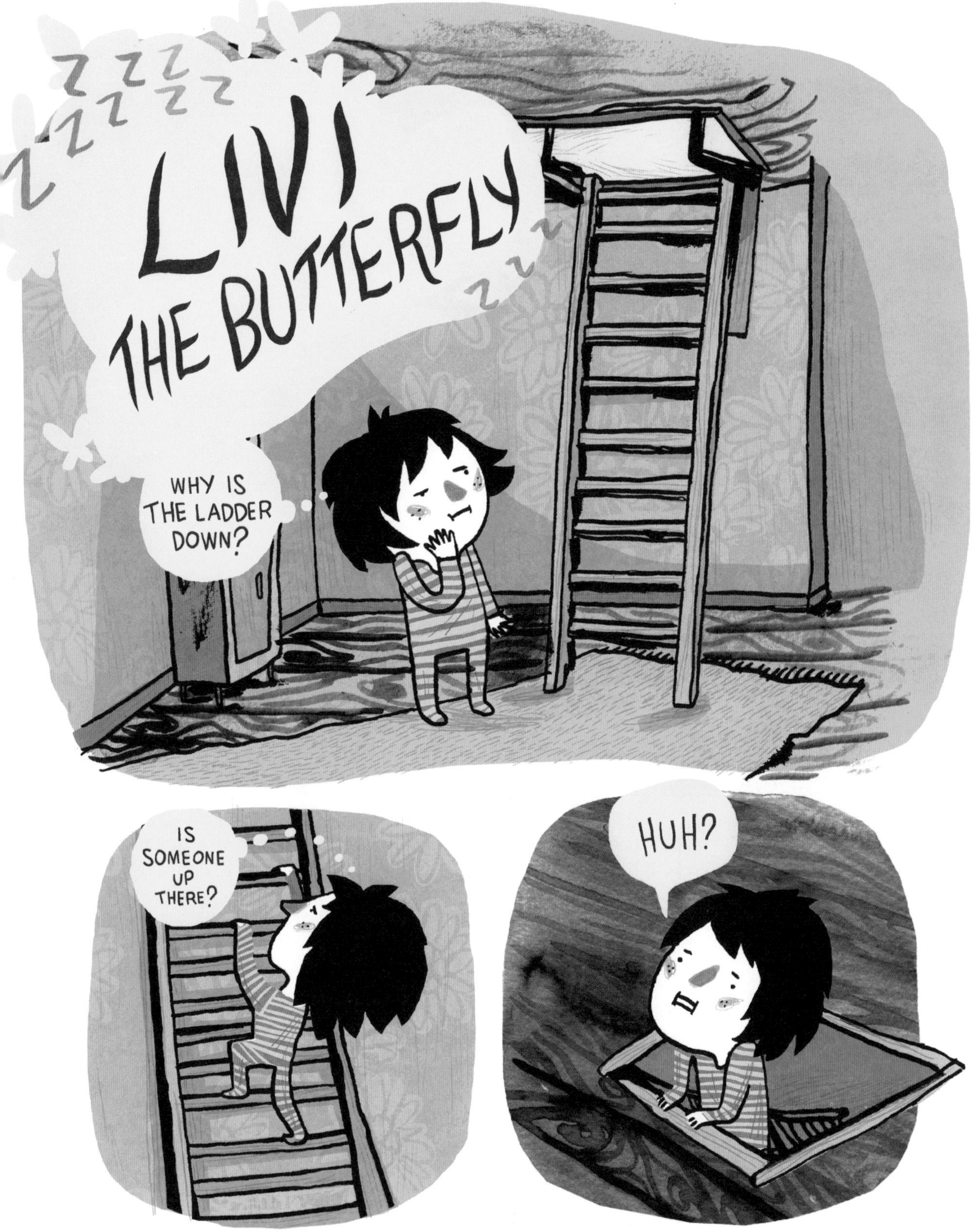
LIVI THE BUTTERFLY
WHY IS THE LADDER DOWN?
IS SOMEONE UP THERE?
HUH?

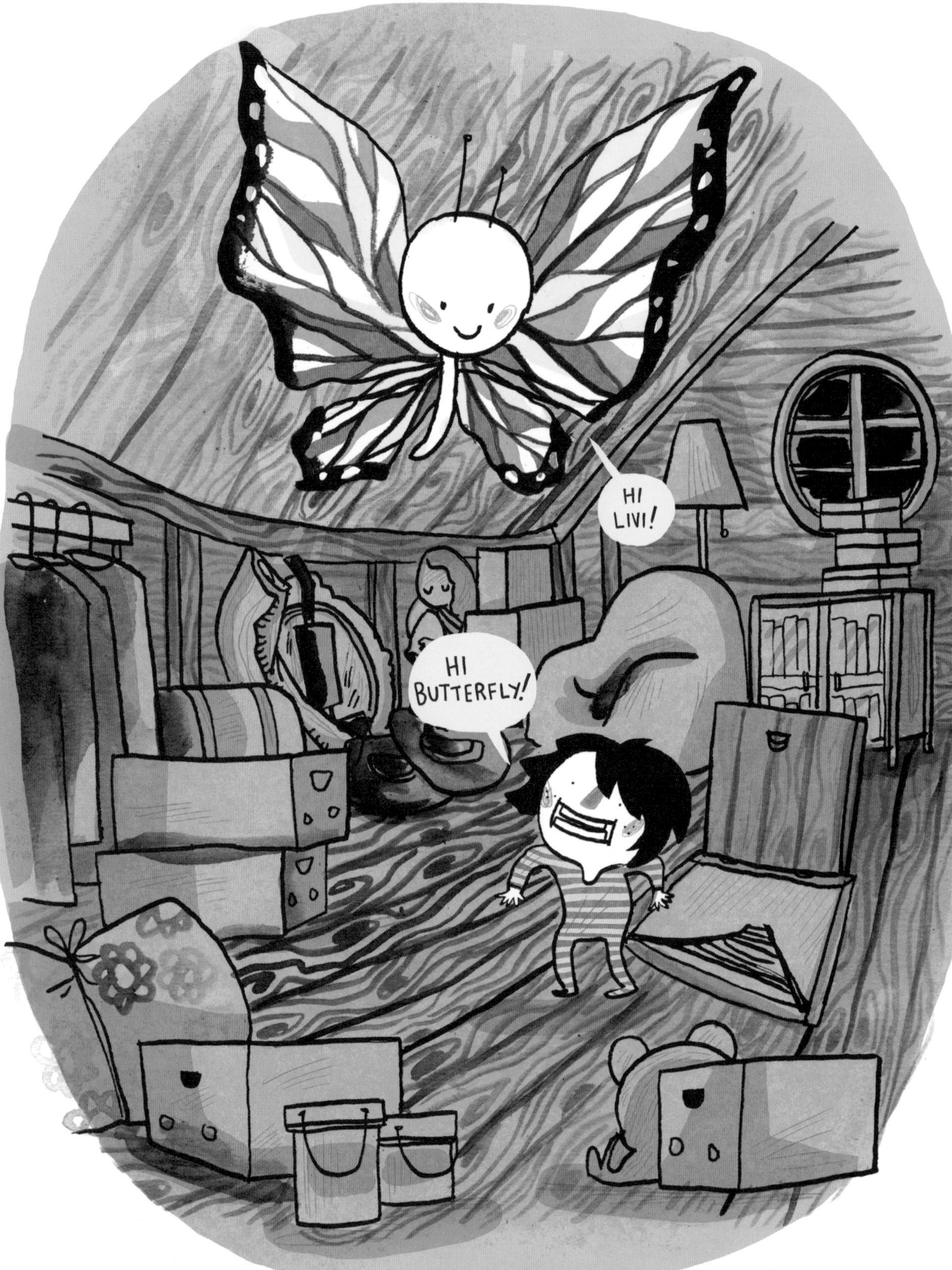
HI LIVI!
HI BUTTERFLY!

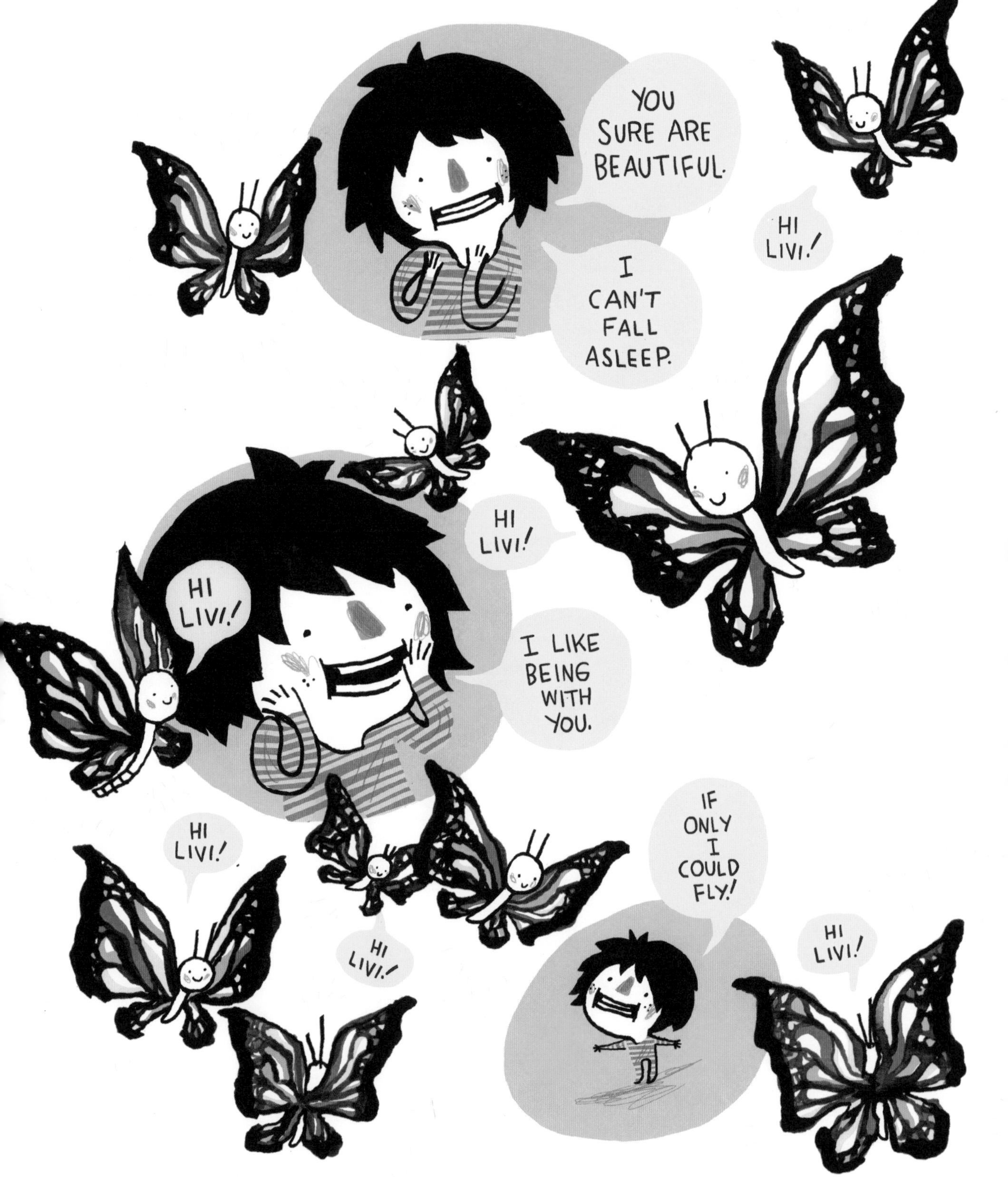
YOU SURE ARE BEAUTIFUL.
HI LIVI!
I CAN'T FALL ASLEEP.
HI LIVI!
HI LIVI!
I LIKE BEING WITH YOU.
HI LIVI!
IF ONLY I COULD FLY!
HI LIVI!
HI LIVI!

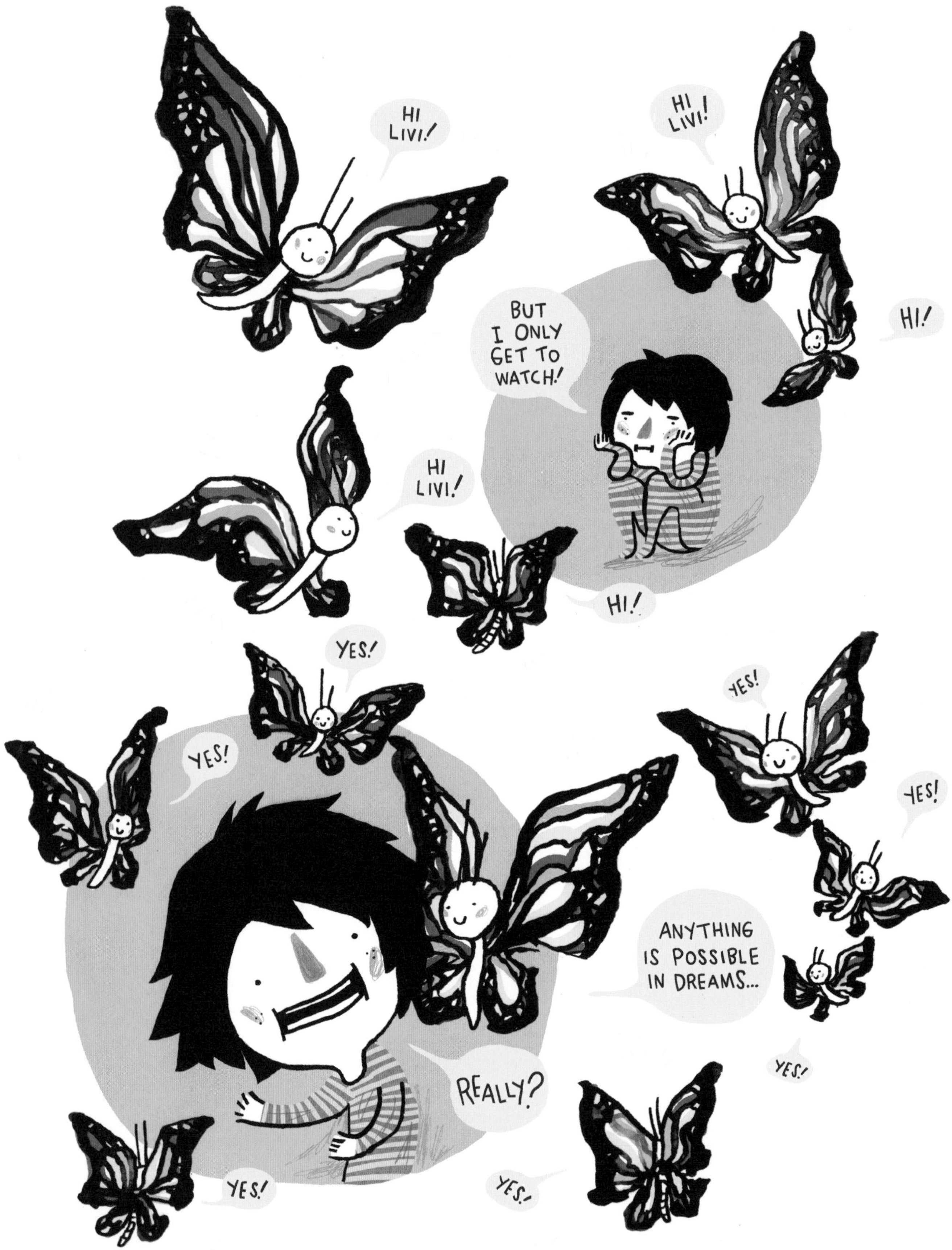
HI LIVI!
HI LIVI!
BUT I ONLY GET TO WATCH!
HI!
HI LIVI!
HI!
YES!
YES!
YES!
YES!
ANYTHING IS POSSIBLE IN DREAMS...
REALLY?
YES!
YES!
YES!

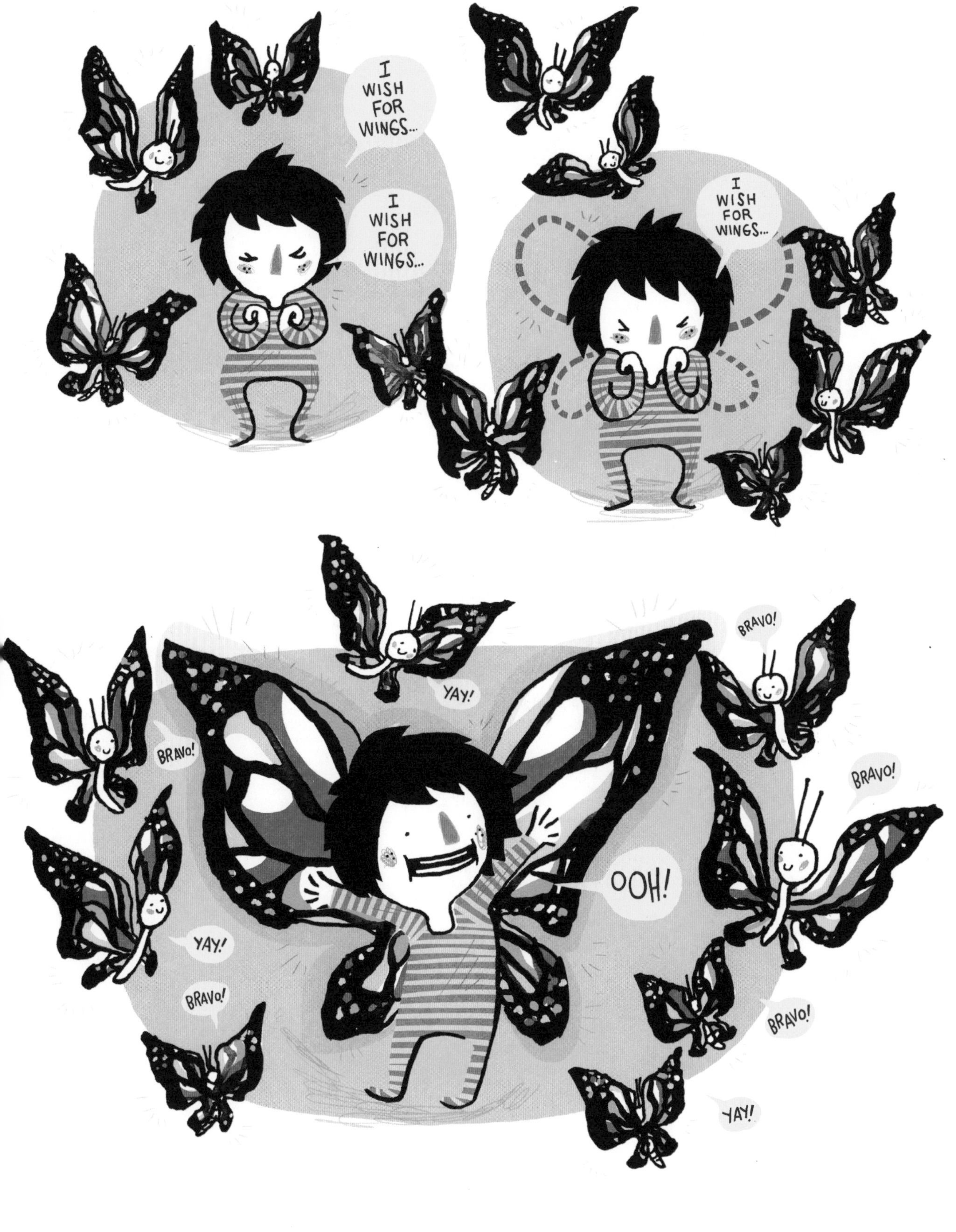
I WISH FOR WINGS...
I WISH FOR WINGS...
I WISH FOR WINGS...
BRAVO!
YAY!
BRAVO!
BRAVO!
OOH!
YAY!
BRAVO!
BRAVO!
YAY!

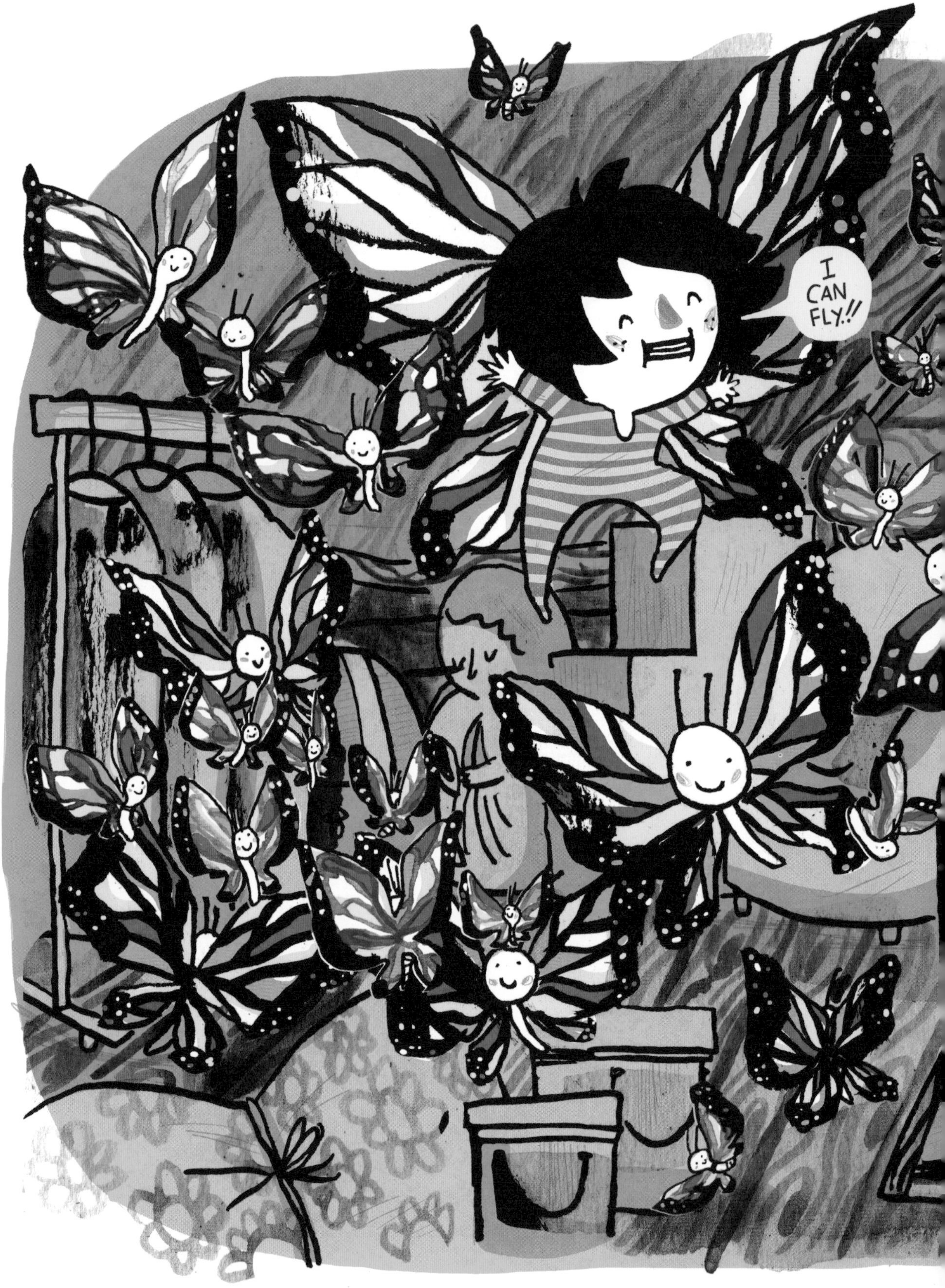
I CAN FLY!!

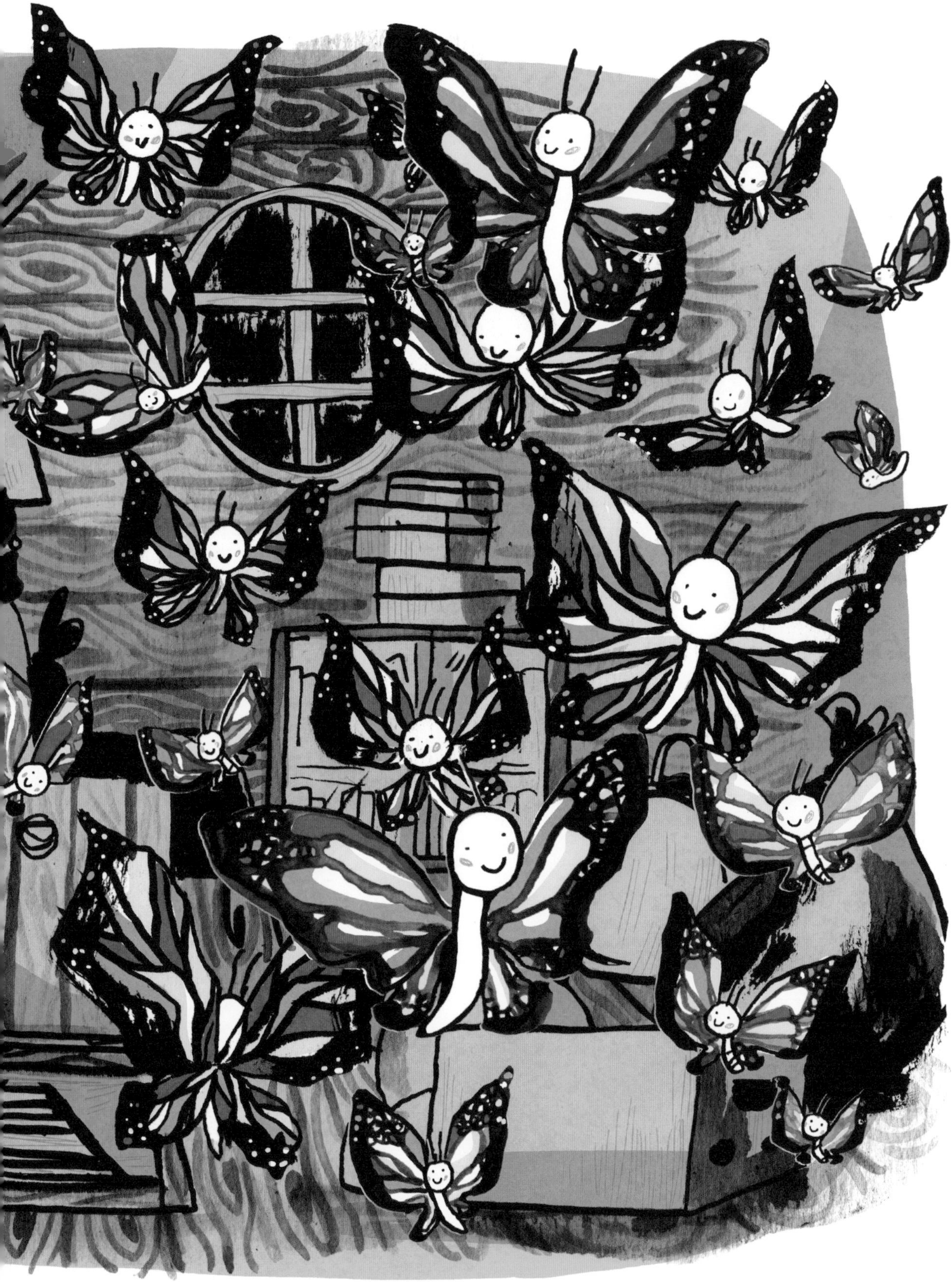

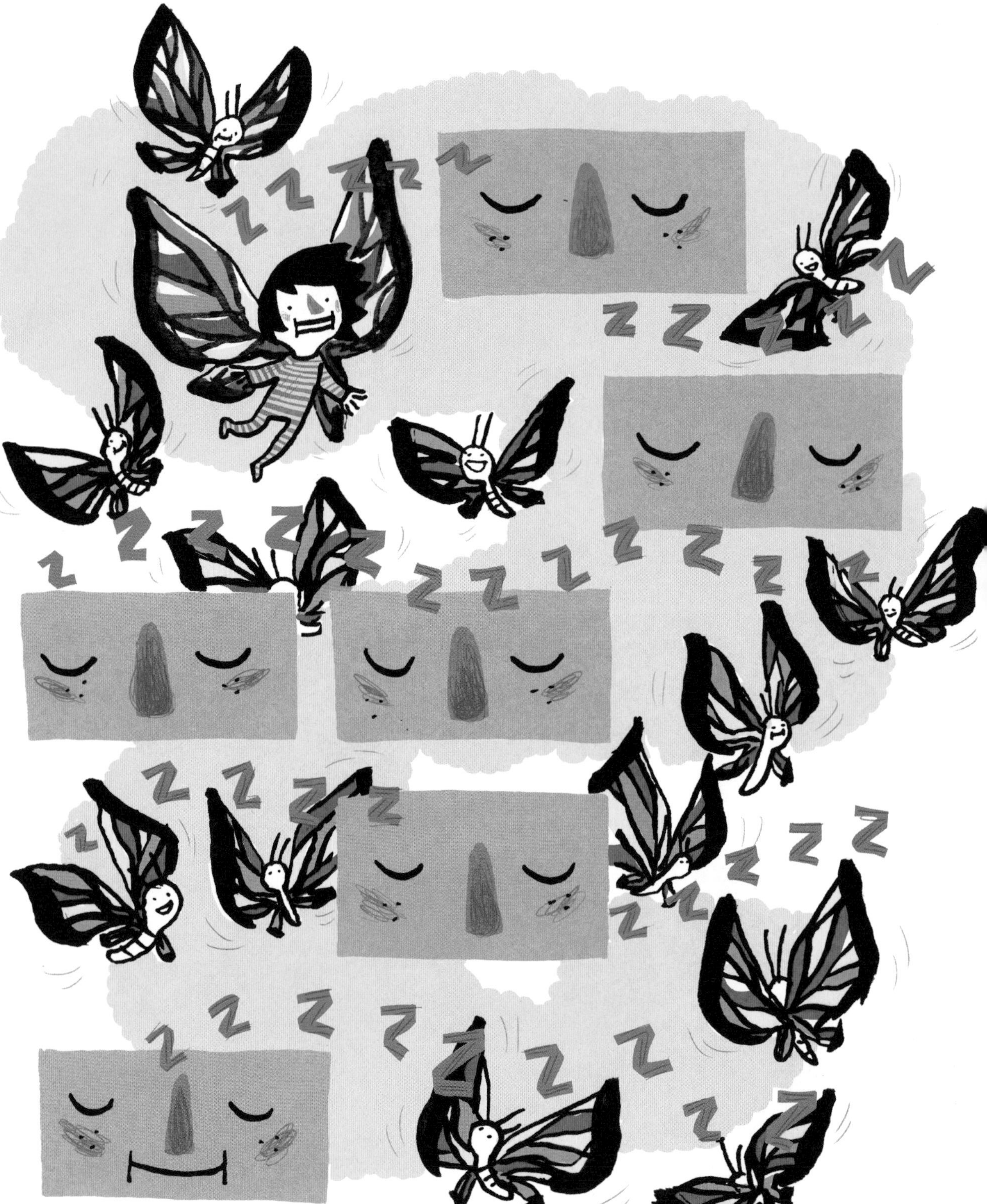

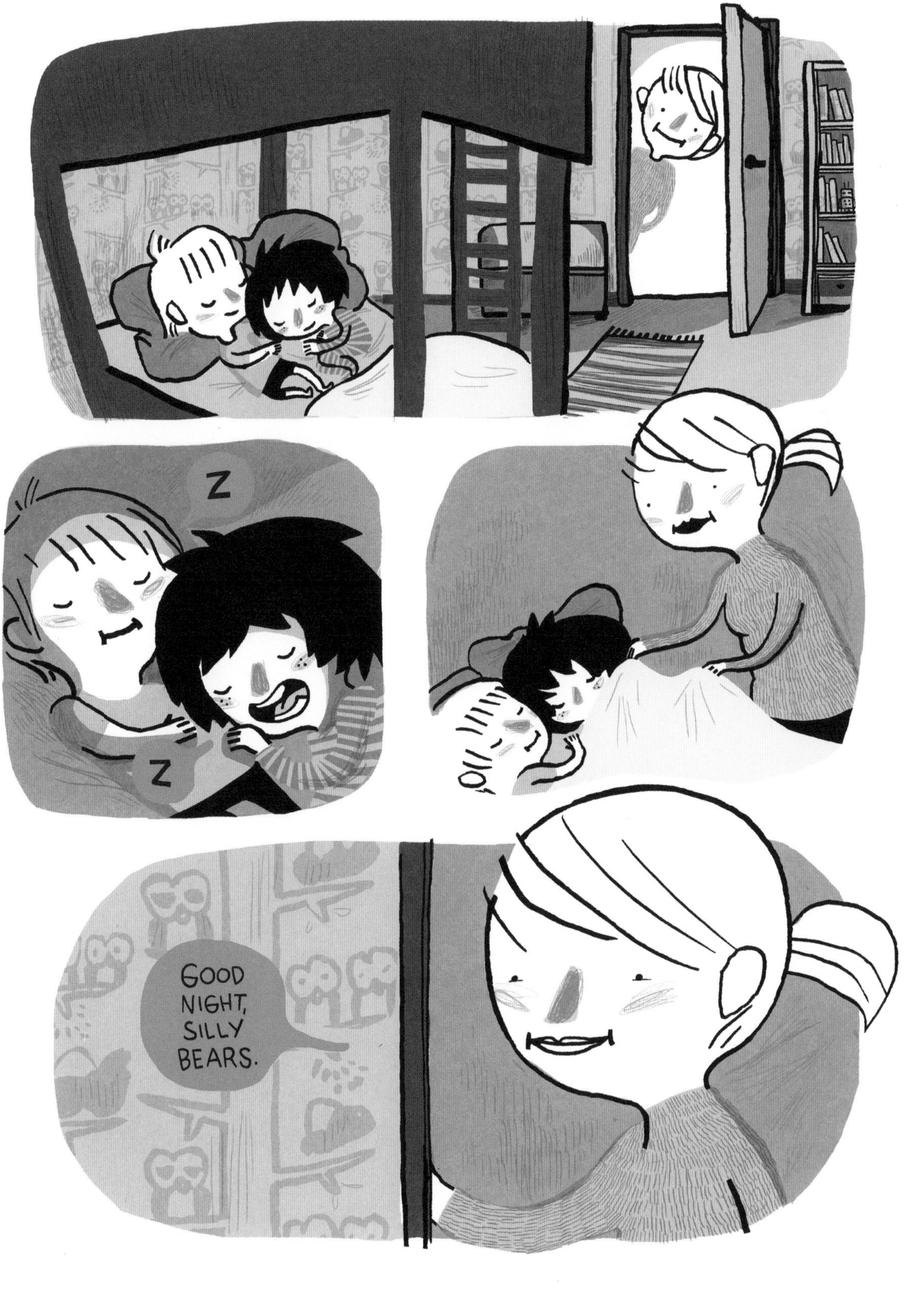
Z
Z
GOOD NIGHT, SILLY BEARS.

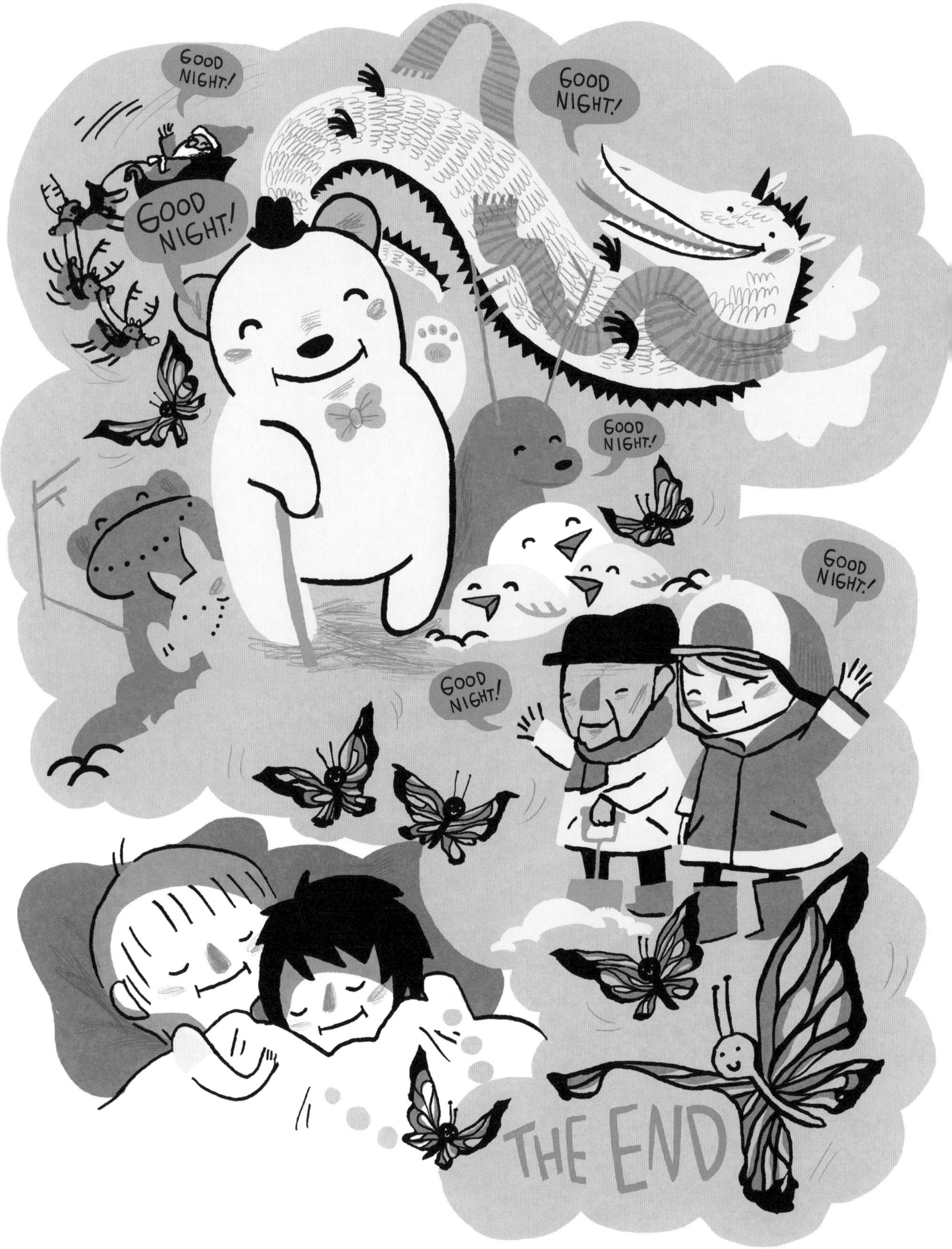
GOOD NIGHT!
GOOD NIGHT!
GOOD NIGHT!
GOOD NIGHT!
GOOD NIGHT!
GOOD NIGHT!
THE END

First published by Kustannusosakeyhtiö Kumiorava as *Sanni ja Joonas–Talviyö* in October 2016

Owlkids Books acknowledges the financial support of the Canada Council for the Arts, the Ontario Arts Council, the Government of Canada through the Canada Book Fund (CBF) and the Government of Ontario through the Ontario Creates Book Initiative for our publishing activities.

Published in Canada by
Owlkids Books Inc.
1 Eglinton Avenue East
Toronto, ON M4P 3A1

Published in the United States by
Owlkids Books Inc.
1700 Fourth Street
Berkeley, CA 94710

Library and Archives Canada Cataloguing in Publication

Title: Livi & Nate / Kalle Hakkola & Mari Ahokoivu ; translated by Owen F. Witesman.
Other titles: Sanni & Joonas, talviyö. English | Livi and Nate
Names: Hakkola, Kalle, author. | Witesman, Owen, translator. | Ahokoivu, Mari, 1984- illustrator.
Description: Translation of: Sanni & Joonas, Talviyö.
Identifiers: Canadiana 20189065826 | ISBN 9781771473729 (hardcover)
Subjects: LCGFT: Graphic novels.
Classification: LCC PZ7.7.H34 Liv 2019 | DDC j741.5/94897—dc23

Library of Congress Control Number: 2018963961

Manufactured in Dongguan, China, in March 2019, by Toppan Leefung Packaging & Printing (Dongguan) Co., Ltd.
Job #BAYDC62

A B C D E F

ONTARIO ARTS COUNCIL
CONSEIL DES ARTS DE L'ONTARIO
an Ontario government agency
un organisme du gouvernement de l'Ontario

Canada Council for the Arts
Conseil des Arts du Canada

Canada

Publisher of Chirp, Chickadee and OWL
www.owlkidsbooks.com

Owlkids Books is a division of bayard canada

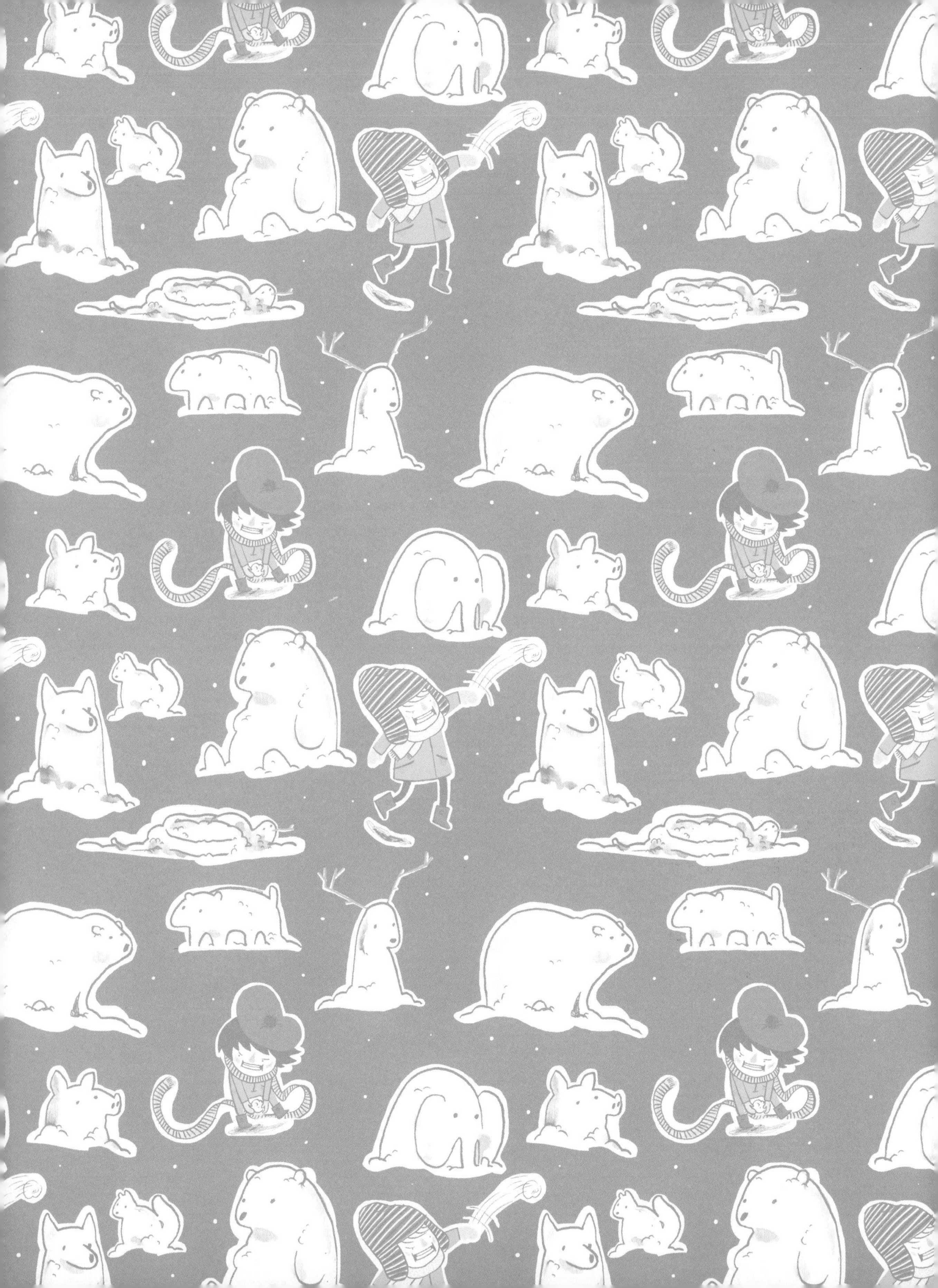